MURDER IN THE HOLY PLACE

Murder in the
Holy Place

LEFT BEHIND
>THE KIDS<

Jerry B. Jenkins

Tim LaHaye

WITH CHRIS FABRY

TYNDALE HOUSE PUBLISHERS, INC.
WHEATON, ILLINOIS

To Rose

TABLE OF CONTENTS

THE YOUNG TRIBULATION FORCE

Original members—Vicki Byrne, Judd Thompson, Lionel Washington

Other members—Mark, Conrad, Darrion, Janie, Charlie, Shelly, Melinda

OTHER BELIEVERS

Jim Dekker—GC satellite operator helping the kids

Chang Wong—Chinese teenager working in New Babylon

Cheryl Tifanne—pregnant young lady from Iowa

Westin Jakes—pilot for singer Z-Van

Tsion Ben-Judah—Jewish scholar who writes about prophecy

Colin and Becky Dial—Wisconsin couple with an underground hideout

Pete Davidson—former biker, now drives a supply truck for the Tribulation Force

Chad Harris—harbors escaped believers in Iowa

Bo and Ginny Shairton, Maggie Carlson, Manny Aguilara—escapees from GC jail

Sam Goldberg—Jewish teenager, Lionel's good friend

Mr. Mitchell Stein—Jewish friend of the Young Trib Force

Chaim Rosenzweig—famous Israeli scientist

UNBELIEVERS

Nicolae Carpathia—leader of the Global Community

Leon Fortunato—Carpathia's right-hand man

Z-Van—lead singer for the popular group, The Four Horsemen

UNDECIDED

Claudia Zander—Morale Monitor, Natalie Bishop's former roommate

What's Gone On Before

VICKI Byrne and the rest of the Young Tribulation Force are living the adventure of a lifetime. When young believers in Iowa send an urgent plea for help, Vicki and the others travel to the GC facility where the kids are being held.

Judd Thompson Jr. and Lionel Washington are alarmed when their teenage friend Chang Wong shows up with dual marks. Though Carpathia's mark was forced on him, Chang despairs and wonders if God will accept him.

In Iowa, their old friend Pete Davidson helps them rescue the believers behind bars before they are forced to take Carpathia's mark. After they escape, Pete leaves, hoping to draw the authorities away from the kids.

Natalie Bishop, a believer working for the Global Community, is discovered by her superior. Vicki hears the news that Natalie has chosen the guillotine rather than take the mark of Carpathia. Later, Natalie's roommate, Claudia Zander, sends an e-mail asking spiritual questions.

Judd and Lionel fly to Israel for the beginning of Nicolae Carpathia's celebration. While in Tel Aviv, they watch a demonstration of Nicolae's latest airplane, piloted by their friend Mac McCullum. The plane crashes and explodes, and Judd fears they have lost more members of the Tribulation Force.

Join the Young Tribulation Force as they enter a time of great deceit and try to tell others the truth about God.

ONE

Death in Tel Aviv

JUDD Thompson Jr. closed his eyes as a plume of smoke rose from the aircraft wreckage less than a mile away. The jet had slammed into the beach at hundreds of miles an hour, followed by a deafening explosion. Judd's ears still rang as he knelt on the beach.

Judd's friend, Mac McCullum, was piloting the plane. Judd tried to imagine the horror of those last few seconds. Chang Wong had told Judd that Mac and a few other believers who worked inside the Global Community were trying to escape. Why hadn't Mac pulled the plane out of the plunge to earth?

A siren sounded from emergency vehicles in the distance, but everyone knew they could send a thousand ambulances to the crater and it wouldn't make any difference. Lionel Washington put a hand on Judd's shoulder.

People near Judd and Lionel, as well as those who surrounded the platform, fell silent. Angry black-and-orange flames billowed from the crash site as the blaze melted the Quasi Two.

A man several feet from them turned to his wife. "I hope they have a record of passengers on that plane. They'll never find any bodies."

The man's wife covered her face. "This was supposed to be such a happy day for the potentate."

Judd looked at Lionel. "The way that thing came down, you think it was sabotage?"

"What do you mean?"

"If somebody found out about Mac and the others, the GC could have made it crash."

Lionel shook his head. "With all these people around? Plus, the plane had equipment for the mark application. They wouldn't have destroyed their own machines."

The eerie silence continued until a woman cried out, "Save them, Potentate!"

Z-Van, the singer Judd and Lionel were traveling with, stood at the back of a group of dignitaries. He leaned forward and spoke to a man in front of him as Nicolae walked to the microphone.

Carpathia held up a hand and tried to soothe the masses with his voice. "Peace be unto you. My peace I give you. Not as the world gives."

Lionel gritted his teeth. "He's ripping off Jesus again."

"Would you please quietly make your way from this place, honoring it as the sacred place of the end for four brave employees. I will ask that the loyalty mark application site be appropriately relocated, and thank you for your reverence during this tragedy."

Z-Van stepped forward, then was ushered off the stage, along with the regional potentates. Leon Fortunato, now the Most High Reverend Father of Carpathianism, stepped to the mike and spread his hands wide. The folds of his robed arms looked like great wings.

"He looks like the most high turkey," Lionel whispered.

Fortunato tried to speak comfortingly to the audience as Carpathia had done, but his voice didn't have the same tone. "Beloved," he said, "while this sadly preempts and concludes today's activities in Tel Aviv, tomorrow's agenda shall remain in place. We look forward to your presence in Jerusalem."

The crowd scattered, some hurrying to automobiles and others standing by the motorcade to get one more look at Carpathia. Bodyguards and officials flanked the man.

Judd and Lionel wandered along the beach to the crash site. The heat from the twisted metal was intense. Global Community security forces had already cordoned off the site with yellow tape. A few people passed, shaking their heads. Some took pictures.

One woman, overcome, laid a bouquet of flowers on the sand. She looked at a friend, wiped away a tear, and said, "They gave their lives in service to the potentate. Those four were heroes."

Judd turned to Lionel as the woman walked away. "Let's get back to Z-Van's plane. I want to call Chang and see if he knows anything about this."

Vicki Byrne rubbed her eyes and looked out at the dark sky. It was early morning in Iowa, and several kids were still awake discussing their next move. Mark and the others agreed that Cheryl Tifanne should accompany them to Wisconsin, but Vicki wanted to go immediately. Colin Dial arrived from one of the other safe houses and joined the discussion.

In the middle of the argument, Mark took a call from Jim Dekker, a believer working inside the Global Community. Mark turned on the speakerphone, and Jim updated them about what had happened since they last talked.

Jim said he was still at the satellite tracking center, searching for any information he could find about Pete. "I know the GC has impounded the van, but I haven't heard anything about Pete. I also know this Commander Fulcire of RAP is in Iowa."

"RAP?" Shelly said.

"The Rebel Apprehension Program," Jim said. "The United North American States have pledged to lead the world in cracking down on anti-Carpathia activity."

"Then they're mostly after believers," Vicki said.

Mark looked at Colin. "Won't they be able to trace your van, the one Pete took?"

Colin shook his head. "We altered the vehicle identification number and assigned it to the GC fleet. I'll call Becky and have her be on alert just in case."

"What about you?" Vicki said. "Why aren't you out of there?"

"I'm not leaving until I know there's nothing I can do to help Pete," Jim said. "There are rumors about us being required to take the mark later today. I want to be out before then."

Vicki asked if Jim knew anything about

Claudia Zander. He didn't but said he would check. When a new report flashed on GCNN, Jim said he would call back soon and hung up.

A news reporter, April Wojekowski, stood on a dark road in Iowa, lights of squad cars flashing behind her. "GCNN has learned of a search for anti-Carpathia forces here in Iowa. We were allowed to fly in with Commander Kruno Fulcire, who wouldn't comment on a possible escape of prisoners at a nearby GC holding facility. But the commander was optimistic that an abandoned van discovered at the side of this road may yield more clues about a possible rebel conspiracy."

Natalie Bishop's picture appeared on the screen and Vicki gasped. Natalie had been accused of helping rebels by using a superior's computer.

The scene switched to April's recorded interview of Commander Fulcire on his plane. "Are there others inside the Global Community who may be helping the rebels?"

Commander Fulcire frowned. "We hope not. That's why we're administering the mark of loyalty as soon as possible to all United North American employees."

"What new measures will you take to capture anti-Carpathia forces?"

Before Fulcire could answer, GCNN

switched live to April again, her hair swirling wildly below a hovering helicopter. She screamed into the microphone to be heard. "We have some activity now in the brush, a few yards from where they discovered the van."

The camera swung to the right, past the television truck, and focused on about a dozen Global Community officers walking through tall brush by the roadside.

"What do you think they found?" Shelly said.

"I just hope it's not Pete," Vicki said.

Judd and Lionel made their way through the lingering crowd in Tel Aviv. Judd had heard there would be as many as 100,000 GC troops brought into Israel, and he did notice more Morale Monitors and Peacekeepers patrolling the streets. Some rode in Jeeps and covered personnel vehicles. Others walked with guns slung over their shoulders. Judd wondered if Carpathia hoped to scare everyone in Israel into following him. If so, Nicolae had greatly misjudged followers of God.

People along the street spoke sadly about the plane crash. Some called it a shame, while others blamed Tsion Ben-Judah. "Some say the thing exploded before it even hit the ground," one man said. "I'll bet the Judah-ites planted a bomb and had it explode over Tel Aviv just to make the potentate look bad."

Some young people sat on sidewalks, dressed in shirts and hats that bore images of The Four Horsemen. They were almost as dejected as Z-Van that his appearance had been cancelled.

Westin Jakes, Z-Van's pilot, came down the stairs of the airplane when Judd and Lionel finally made it to the airport. Westin had become a believer soon after Nicolae Carpathia's rise from the dead.

"I don't mean to spoil the party," Westin said, "but I don't advise you guys riding with us. It's not a pretty sight back there."

"What's wrong?" Lionel said.

No sooner had Lionel spoken than a guitar flew out the open door, spinning down the stairs, and smashing onto the tarmac. Z-Van screamed and cursed at someone inside.

"Who's he mad at?" Lionel said.

"Everybody," Westin said. "Join me in the cockpit."

Judd and Lionel quickly ran up the steps and slipped into the cockpit.

Z-Van screamed from the back of the plane, "We had the potentate right there! We

were all ready, and because of this airplane
foul-up, we have to reschedule!"

Someone spoke softly and Z-Van screamed
again. "I swear, Lars, if you film any of this
I'll throw the camera twice as far as I threw
the guitar."

"That film guy still following Z-Van
around?" Lionel whispered.

Westin nodded. "They were set to shoot
the songs at the platform, but the plane crash
wiped their schedule."

Judd fumed. "I can't believe he's more
concerned about singing his new songs than
he is about the people killed in the crash."

Westin cocked his head. "That's my boss."

Westin turned on a tiny monitor and tuned
in the GCNN station in Tel Aviv. They had
been showing the live broadcast of the festivi-
ties up to the crash of the plane. Two grim-
faced anchors played amateur video that
showed the best moments of the fatal flight.

Westin scowled. "The way that thing came
down tells me there was a major problem."

"What do you mean?" Judd said.

"You have all those acrobatic moves, all
the fancy flyovers, and then everything goes
blank. The pilot doesn't even try to pull out."

"Maybe he couldn't," Judd said.

A photo of Mac McCullum flashed on the

screen. The news anchor said, "We now have confirmed those members of the flight crew and the two passengers. Captain Mac McCullum was said to be one of the Global Community's most experienced pilots, the person who usually flew Potentate Carpathia's plane, the Phoenix 216. He is presumed dead, along with copilot Abdullah Smith, a former Jordanian fighter pilot and first officer for the Global Community."

The news anchor paused. "We should be reminded that there are perhaps family members of these victims who are just now finding out about their loved ones' deaths, and for that we apologize.

"Also among the dead, this woman, Hannah Palemoon. Originally from the United North American States, she was a nurse by profession, so one can assume she may have been on the flight to help administer the mark of loyalty here in Tel Aviv.

"Perhaps the most shocking casualty was a director in Potentate Carpathia's cabinet, David Hassid. We understand he was one of the technical geniuses who helped behind the scenes in New Babylon. I'm sure His Excellency will miss the input of these colleagues, and again, our hearts go out to those who are family members and those who knew the deceased."

Z-Van threw open the cockpit door and rushed inside. "Get me back to Jerusalem!" He eyed Judd and Lionel and cursed again. "And get these two off my plane."

Westin started his preflight procedures and said, "Sir, we promised them—"

"I don't care what you or I or anybody else promised. I want them off and I don't want them back on. Understood?"

"Yes, sir," Westin said.

Vicki and the others sat engrossed in the GCNN coverage of the situation in Iowa. Periodically the news switched to Israel to report on the plane crash that had taken four lives. Vicki whimpered when Mac McCullum's picture appeared. The kids knew Mac was a member of the Tribulation Force.

The phone rang and Mark picked up as the kids continued to monitor the news. His eyes darted around the room. When he hung up he looked at Vicki. "If we're getting out of here, we should do it now. Jim said the GC is converging. He sent an urgent message that a small convoy was fleeing south toward Kansas City. He thinks that'll give us enough time to get on the road back to Wisconsin."

"Is he getting out?" Vicki said.

"As soon as he knows we're safe," Mark said.

"Let's go," Colin Dial said, grabbing a few of their belongings.

"Wait," Shelly said. "The van's gone."

"Take my family's minivan," Chad Harris said from the shadows.

Vicki turned to the young man and smiled. Chad had helped her deal with Natalie's death. She put a hand on his arm. "Thank you for being here when we needed you."

Chad nodded. "I hate to see you go, but you'll always have a place here if you need it." He took Vicki's hand, then hugged her.

Conrad yelled and the kids rushed back to the television. The reporter was excitedly announcing that after an exhaustive search, Global Community authorities had found something about a hundred yards from the road. The camera zoomed into the darkness where two uniformed officers dragged someone through the brush.

"It appears to be a large man," April Wojekowski said.

Vicki put a hand to her mouth as the group approached. Between the two GC officers was her friend Pete.

TWO

Z-Van's Revenge

VICKI looked closely at the television, trying to see Pete. As the GC officers dragged him past squad cars, she noticed how pale he was. A large, red stain spread through Pete's shirt.

Commander Fulcire moved in front of the camera and barked orders. The officers dragged Pete toward the chopper.

The reporter, April, touched the commander's shoulder. "Sir, how did you make this arrest?"

"The chopper can see anything on the ground giving off heat," Fulcire said. "Without the chopper, we'd have never found him in that clump of bushes."

The camera focused on Pete, and the commander waved April through. It was clear they had worked out an agreement about this exclusive story.

"We have to go," Colin said from the top of the stairs.

"Let Vicki watch," Mark said.

Vicki knelt in front of the television, too stunned to cry. She had met Pete after the great wrath of the Lamb earthquake, as the kids were trying to escape from another GC commander. Pete had always been kind to Vicki, willing to listen or help. She knew God had changed him drastically, and it was difficult watching his arrest.

Vicki had hoped Pete would find a way out with another trucker, or perhaps locate a motorcycle or another vehicle. Now, as the officers trudged past a squad car, she knew her friend was in deep trouble.

The reporter thrust a microphone in front of Pete and yelled, "Sir, do you have anything to say?"

"Yeah, I sure do." The camera zoomed in on Pete's face. His hair was matted and filled with grass, his face streaked with mud. Vicki guessed Pete had tried to camouflage himself in the underbrush. She could only imagine what had gone through his mind as he lay bleeding, wet, and cold, watching the lights of the oncoming GC.

Pete caught his breath and looked into the camera. "Everybody watching needs to know that if they take Carpathia's mark, they'll regret it for eternity."

April pulled the microphone away, but Pete grabbed it. "Jesus Christ is the true potentate. Ask him to forgive you!"

The officers wrestled the microphone from Pete and threw him on the ground. Pete yelled out the address to Tsion Ben-Judah's Web site as they restrained him.

The reporter composed herself. "Well, that's not a surprising response from an avowed Judah-ite. As we've been told, these fanatics will stop at nothing to push their beliefs on others."

Pete was led to the chopper and shoved inside.

Mark touched Vicki's shoulder. "We should leave."

Vicki nodded. It wasn't until she was in the van, driving away, that the tears finally came.

Judd stood and motioned Lionel to follow as Z-Van left the cockpit.

Westin shook his head. "I can't let him treat you guys like this."

"It's okay," Judd said. "We'll find a ride to Jerusalem."

"But I have to leave him sooner or later. Why not now?"

Judd stared at Westin. "When the time's right, you'll know."

Westin handed Judd a wad of cash. "You can pay me back later. Look me up at Ben Gurion airport. I promised you a ride back to the States and I'm going to keep my word, no matter what he says."

Westin grabbed a cell phone from a compartment behind him and handed it to Judd. "It's solar powered. My number is the first one on the list. Call me if you have any problems."

Judd and Lionel shook hands with Westin and headed for the stairs. When they were halfway down, Z-Van yelled at them from the doorway. His eyes seemed on fire and his face was tight with anger. "I'm going to tell them about you."

Judd nodded. "I figured you would."

"I could have given you up in New Babylon if I wanted."

"Why didn't you?"

Z-Van smirked. "I thought I could get you two to see the truth. I was going to make you GC poster children, you know, two kids who were once Judah-ites who did a 180. I was going to prove to everybody that people like you could be rehabilitated."

"I guess there's just no hope for us," Judd said.

Z-Van clenched his teeth. "You'll regret not turning. You'll see how powerful His Excellency is in Jerusalem. I know what he's going to do, and it'll prove once and for all how wrong you are."

Judd took another step down the stairs. "We know what he's going to do too, and all it's going to prove is that Nicolae is the enemy of the true God."

Z-Van waved a hand, dismissing them, and went back inside.

When Judd and Lionel reached the terminal, the jet engines fired. The cell phone in Judd's pocket rang and he answered it.

"I just heard Z-Van on the phone with airport security," Westin said. "Get out of there as fast as you can."

Judd quickly told Lionel what Westin had said. Since there was a fence around the runway, they had to go through the terminal. They rushed inside to the baggage claim area and ducked into a men's room.

Judd checked the stalls and made sure they were alone. "They'll be looking for two of us. Let's split up and meet out front."

"I wonder what Z-Van told them we did," Lionel said.

"He's probably ticked that we don't worship Carpathia like he does."

"Yeah, his album sales would go in the tank if everybody was a believer."

Lionel walked out first and went to the right. Moments later, Judd walked out and turned left. He noticed a security guard standing watch by the door leading to the tarmac. Judd stared straight ahead and kept walking.

Judd spied three airport officials with walkie-talkies at the escalator leading upstairs to the street level. He turned into a hallway and found a wall of vending machines. As he put in a few coins, a radio crackled.

"Yes, we heard you," a man said, "one black, one white, and they're together. Do you have a description of their clothing?"

A candy bar fell with a clunk to the bottom of the machine, and Judd heard a noise down the hall. A cleaning woman exited a service elevator pushing a cart.

Judd raced toward her and managed to slip inside before the door closed. *I hope Lionel made it out okay*, he thought.

Judd pushed the button for the main floor, but nothing happened. He pushed other buttons, but the lights remained unlit. He was about to hit the Door Open button when the car shook and slowly moved upward. When it reached the main floor,

Judd slid to the side and waited as another cleaning person walked inside.

Judd darted out the door and was down the hall before the man stuck his head out and said, "Hey, you're not supposed to use this."

Judd turned the corner and walked into the crowded terminal. Directly ahead was a row of exits, each with a security guard poised and watching. Several young men had been pulled out of line, so Judd kept moving, hoping he wouldn't see Lionel in custody.

When he reached the end of the concourse, he glanced outside and noticed Lionel beside a small car, looking anxiously toward the terminal. Judd checked the exits again and spotted an emergency door at the far side of the room that led directly outside. Judd figured he would have no problem reaching Lionel before the guards realized what was happening, so he moved toward it, reading the sign on the lever that said, Attention: Alarm Will Sound If Door Is Opened.

Judd took a breath and hit the door running. Alarms rang throughout the concourse and a red light he hadn't noticed swirled overhead. Whistles sounded behind him as Judd sprinted toward Lionel.

Lionel jumped in the back of the small car, pulled Judd in with him, and yelled, "Go!"

The driver was a short, Middle Eastern man, with graying hair and glasses. He turned to Judd and stuck out his hand as he pulled into heavy traffic. Judd shook it quickly, startled at the speed of the oncoming cars. Airport officials ran toward the street, but the car blended into traffic before they could reach it.

"I didn't mean to scare you," the driver said. Judd noticed the mark of the believer on his forehead. "My name is Sabir. It is nice to meet you, believer Judd. I will drive you to Jerusalem."

Vicki sat in the backseat of the van with Cheryl. The only sound during the first few minutes of the drive was the sniffling of the kids. Mark rode with Colin in front, checking their route with Jim Dekker by phone. Shelly had her head on Conrad's shoulder in the middle seat, wiping away tears.

As the sun slowly appeared over the horizon, everyone relaxed a little and ate sandwiches their friends in Iowa had made.

"What will happen to the other kids who came from the reeducation facility?" Cheryl said.

"They're safe in people's homes if they stay

put," Colin said. "I was staying at a place with a secret subbasement where the guys stayed. Even if the GC did house-to-house searches, I doubt they'd find them."

Conrad checked the latest on the Web from the laptop. News of the plane crash in Tel Aviv was the top story. The world awaited the special ceremony in Israel the following day.

Cheryl put a hand on Vicki's shoulder. "I'm really sorry about your friend. What's going to happen?"

"They'll probably question him, and when they're done, they'll offer him the mark of Carpathia."

"But you said people shouldn't take it."

"Pete won't. And he won't tell them anything about us, no matter what they do."

"He did that for us, just like Jesus gave himself," Cheryl said, looking out the window at the passing landscape. "You know, I was really upset about being caught by the GC, but the way I see it now, it's probably the best thing that's ever happened to me."

Vicki smiled. "When we get to Wisconsin, we'll see if Colin's wife can find you some prenatal vitamins."

"What are those?"

"You take them so your baby will be strong and healthy."

Cheryl gave her a pained smile and glanced out the window again.

"You want to talk about it?" Vicki said.

"There's not much to tell. I grew up in an orphanage. I never knew my mother and father, but I always felt like they didn't want me. I was sixteen when the disappearances happened. We woke up and most of the workers were gone. Little kids too.

"Later, I moved into an apartment with three girlfriends who were older and going to school. That's when I met Thomas. He was a student at the university, and I loved him." She frowned. "I thought he loved me."

"What happened?"

"A month ago, I was out looking for work. I had lost my job. I went to his apartment and it was empty. He had left a note with one of my roommates saying that he was moving back in with his family, and that I shouldn't look for him. I felt so alone and betrayed."

Cheryl put her head in her hands. "My roommates laughed at me for believing Thomas could love me. I laughed along with them at first, but I couldn't take it anymore and decided to leave."

"Where did you go?"

"I lived on the streets for a while. Ate in soup kitchens and GC shelters. A few days ago I wandered into this grocery store without any

money, which was a mistake. I smelled the
fresh-baked bread and I had to have a bagel or
something. I stuffed a couple in my pockets
and I guess somebody saw me. They caught
me outside and the GC brought me to that
reeducation place. I was glad to have something to eat, but it wasn't much fun.

"That's when those girls started talking
about God. I was drawn to them because
they seemed to have so much love. Then I
wondered if I was believing for the wrong
reasons. You know, that I just wanted a
family and somebody to love me so much
that I'd fall for anything. But when you told
me those verses and how God loved me,
something happened I can't explain. I knew
what you were saying was true."

Vicki smiled. "When I prayed with you and
saw you didn't have the mark, I was really
scared. I'm glad you're part of our family
now."

"I want to learn as much as I can and help
other people know the truth," Cheryl said.
She paused.

"What is it?"

"I don't want to be a bad influence on
your friends."

"You mean the baby?" Vicki said.

Cheryl nodded.

"We've all made mistakes. Big ones. God loves each of us, and he loves your child too."

Vicki scooted closer. She had been thinking about Cheryl's baby since she had heard the girl was pregnant. "Have you thought of what you're going to do after the child is born?"

Cheryl winced. "It's all so new. . . ."

Vicki wanted to tell Cheryl about the two boys she had been thinking of, but she had no idea why the names *Ben* and *Brad* had stuck in her head. "If there were someone who might want to take care of your baby, would you consider it?"

"Who?"

Vicki frowned. "Honestly, I don't know. But would you be open to an adoption?"

Cheryl smiled. "If you think it's a good idea, I'll consider it."

As the minivan rumbled through the back roads of Iowa, Vicki racked her brain thinking about the two boys. She ran through the faces of everyone she had met in the past few years. From Chloe Williams to Hattie Durham to her teachers at Nicolae High, she could think of no one with those names.

THREE

Sabir's Story

JUDD kept watch behind them for signs of Global Community officers, but Sabir knew the roads well and was soon traveling through parts of Israel neither Judd nor Lionel had seen before.

"How did you get out of the airport?" Judd said to Lionel.

"I saw an African-American couple and started up a conversation. I went through the front doors with them, and I hoped security would think I was with them. They weren't checking families."

Judd explained how he had found the service elevator and eluded the guards. "I don't know what Z-Van said, but they sure seemed anxious to get us."

"You were with Z-Van?" Sabir said. "The one who screams and calls it music?"

Judd smiled and looked at the man's eyes in the rearview mirror. He seemed kind and good-humored, and Judd wondered what he had gone through in the past three and a half years. "If you think Z-Van's music is bad, wait until you hear the new tune Leon Fortunato wants you to sing."

"You mean 'Hail Carpathia'? I've already heard it and have a different version."

Lionel chuckled. "You came up with new lyrics?"

In his soft voice, Sabir sang the melody to 'Hail Carpathia' with a mocking twist.

> *Hey, Carpathia, you're not the risen*
> *king;*
> *Hey, Carpathia, you don't rule anything.*
> *We'll worship God until we die*
> *And fight against you, Nicolae.*
> *Hey, Carpathia, you're not the risen*
> *king.*

Judd laughed. As Sabir sang again, Judd thought about some of his old high school friends and how they had laughed together at television programs and movies. With the death and destruction in the world, that carefree spirit was gone. In fact, Judd couldn't remember when he had laughed this hard. It wasn't the humor in the words, but the tone of Sabir's voice, his perfect imitation of Leon Fortunato, and the way he waved his arm over the steering wheel like he was leading a thousand-voice choir.

One of Judd's favorite phrases, that always angered his father, was "Lighten up!" Judd recalled times when his father's business wasn't going well and his dad appeared weighed down with responsibilities. Now, Judd felt that same weight. He knew there would be a time when he could laugh freely again, and this brief chuckle was a taste of what was to come.

When Sabir finished his concert, Judd asked why he was going to Jerusalem.

The man shrugged. "To take you there, of course."

"Why were you at the airport?"

Sabir smiled. "I live not far from there. Sometimes I feel God tells me to go there. Other times I park and pray for the people I see and try to find a believer or two and encourage them."

"What about today?" Lionel said. "Did God tell you to come there?"

Sabir shook his head. "I was listening to

coverage of Carpathia's arrival on the radio. It grieved me that so many were going to take his mark of loyalty, and I wanted to pray for them. I drove around the site asking God to show people the truth and wound up at the airport."

"So you're making a special trip just for us?" Judd said.

"You would do the same for me if I had come to your country, would you not?"

Judd nodded. "I hope I would."

Sabir pointed out some of the ancient sites as they passed, and Judd was amazed at the history of the country. Finally, he asked how Sabir had become a believer in Jesus Christ.

Sabir winced. "For that story, I have to tell you some terrible things about myself."

Vicki listened to more of Cheryl's story. The girl seemed hungry to learn about the Bible, and Vicki gave a quick overview of the Scriptures. Cheryl asked Conrad and Shelly to tell their stories, and the two joined the discussion.

When it was Vicki's turn, she described meeting Judd and the others in the Young

Tribulation Force after the disappearances. She told Cheryl that it was a pastor, Bruce Barnes, who had explained the truth to her and the other kids.

"Now that I understand what God did for me, I want to tell other people," Cheryl said. "Did that happen to you?"

Vicki smiled. "Absolutely. I couldn't believe people at Nicolae High couldn't see the truth. One of the first people I talked to about God was . . ." Vicki stopped and stared off.

"What is it?" Cheryl said.

"I just remembered something. A woman whose husband was a police officer wanted to know why all the children had disappeared."

Now Vicki had Conrad's attention. "What are you talking about?"

"Fogarty. Josey Fogarty was her name. Her husband was Tom. Judd and I helped him catch a couple of crooks."

"Did Josey become a believer?" Cheryl said.

Vicki nodded. "I remember I wished Bruce would come and talk with her, but she wanted to pray with me."

"What about her?" Shelly said.

"She told me she had been into all kinds of religions and some weird stuff when she got divorced from her first husband. She lost custody of her two kids."

"But why is she important—?"

Vicki put a hand on Shelly's shoulder. "She had two sons who disappeared. Their names were Ben and Brad."

Judd sat riveted to Sabir's story as they drove toward Jerusalem. Sabir said that before the disappearances, he had been a terrorist.

"I grew up in a community that hates all Jewish people, just like Carpathia. He hates Jews even though he signed the peace treaty with them. Our religious leaders believed that God would reward us for actions against Israelis, and so we plotted terrible acts."

"You tried to kill them?" Lionel said.

"Yes. Looking back, I can't believe I did some of those things. I actually taught people, some younger than you, how to use explosives and blow themselves up in buses, on sidewalks, or other crowded places. The goal was to kill as many people as possible, and we did it in the name of God."

Judd had read the history of violence in the Middle East, particularly in Israel. During the time before the Rapture, there had been many attempts at peace, some of which seemed like real breakthroughs, but no sooner was a treaty signed than the violence broke out again and people were killed. But the peace treaty signed by Carpathia brought a new era to the world. Judd knew it was only the lull before the storm of Carpathia's wrath against Jewish people.

"Why did you stop the bombing and violence?" Lionel said.

"Because I learned the truth about God. I love my family and my culture, but I discovered the God who created me is a God of love, and the Jewish people have a special place in his kingdom. Now I love them with all my heart, and I pray that they will turn to their Messiah."

"How did you go from wanting to blow them up to loving them?" Judd said.

Sabir smiled. "That is a question many in my family continue to ask. Though I have tried to explain, they do not understand."

Sabir merged with traffic and found the main route between Tel Aviv and Jerusalem. "I had never questioned whether I was doing the right thing when I helped plan killings. I was taught to hate from the time I was a boy. We learned songs that glorified violence, we thought God was on our side, and that we would gain special favors in heaven for sacrificing ourselves."

"You actually planned the killings?" Lionel said.

"I trained many young assassins and helped build explosive devices." Sabir ran a hand through his hair. "My own son, not much older than you, died in a terrible explosion I planned. Sometimes I have nightmares about him and the others I sent to their deaths."

"But didn't you feel bad about the people you killed?" Judd said.

"A terrorist cannot afford sympathy. It is the same as being a coward. That's how we were trained."

"If you were convinced you were right, what changed your mind?" Judd said. "It must have been miraculous."

Sabir nodded and smiled. "It was about three years ago and I had been having trouble sleeping. My wife—I wish you could meet her—had been reading everything about the disappearances she could find. There were magazine articles and, of course, theories by the Global Community. She was interested in the possibility that God had taken his people to heaven. I told her it was a foolish idea. We were still on earth and we were God's faithful.

"One night, I tossed and turned on my bed, unable to sleep. I went to the roof of our home and sat outside, looking at the stars. I must have dozed off, but I suddenly saw a man in a white robe standing on the other side of a body of water. He motioned for me to come to him and said my religion did not follow the truth.

"Understand, I'm not saying God spoke directly to me. Some people have based their faith on some kind of vision and have been very wrong. This message caused me to investigate Jesus and do something I had never done before—read the Bible."

"What did your wife think?" Judd said.

"I woke her and told her what had happened. We found a Web site that talked of Jesus. I found a Bible on-line and read the prophecies he fulfilled. We both knelt by our computer and asked God to forgive us. As you can see by the mark on my forehead, he did."

"What did your friends say?"

Sabir pulled the collar of his shirt down, revealing an ugly scar. "They nearly killed me. My wife and I put everything we owned in this car and drove to the Old City. I had plotted against the lives of so many Jewish people, and I was going into that city looking for help. That's when another great miracle occurred."

Vicki told the others more about Josey
Fogarty. Cheryl asked if Josey's husband had
become a believer.

Vicki pursed her lips. "I'm not sure. One of
his friends on the police force died and Judd
tried to convince him of the truth, but I never
heard what happened."

"And you think this woman would take
care of my baby?"

"All I can tell you is that those two little
boys' names came to mind when I heard
about your situation. I think Josey would be
a great mom, but we'd have to find her and
ask."

Vicki dialed the safe house in Wisconsin
and spoke with Colin's wife, Becky. When
Darrion came on the line, Vicki gave her all
the information about Josey she could think
of and asked Darrion to do a search for her.

"I'll give it my best shot," Darrion said.

"What happened in Jerusalem?" Judd said,
scooting forward so he could hear Sabir
better.

The man put both hands on the wheel and
stretched. "When I think of it now, I see it as

a great answer to prayer and a sign from a loving God that he cares for his children. My wife and I drove through the streets late that night. But what were we looking for? Someone, anyone, who believed in Jesus as Messiah. And how would we find such a person? The Orthodox Jews hate even the mention of his name."

Judd tried to put himself in the man's place. Sabir and his wife had turned their backs on everything they had followed their whole lives.

"I pulled to a stop at the side of a narrow street and my wife and I prayed that God would show us where to go. A man walked by and I asked if there was a church nearby. I figured I might find a believer there.

"The man laughed at me and said there were plenty of churches, but that no one would be at any of them that time of night. He pointed out the Church of the Holy Sepulchre. I had no idea of the history of that place. I simply needed help.

"We parked and walked there. The man was correct—the church was locked tight, so we sat outside near the front, our heads in our hands, and prayed."

Sabir wiped his eyes and continued. "A few moments later we heard footsteps, and someone came out of the dark and stood only a few feet from us. He said, 'Have you come to find the way?' I asked him what way he was talking about. The man, his name was Ezra, knelt before us and said, 'He is risen.' I knew then that he was a believer in the true Christ.

"But I felt like the man should know who he was helping. I told him what I have told you, that I had plotted to kill Jews and that I was guilty of many deaths. With tears in his eyes he said, 'Have you asked God to forgive you, and have you accepted the forgiveness he offers in the Lord Jesus?' I broke down and told him we both had."

Sabir's shoulders shook, and Judd thought the man was going to run off the road. When he had composed himself, Judd said, "What did the man do?"

"He told me that his wife and two children had been killed in an attack in Ramallah a few years earlier. It was one I had planned."

"Did you tell him that?" Judd said.

"I had to. I told him how sorry I was, but he stopped me, grabbed my hand, raised me to my feet, and hugged me. 'You have been forgiven by God and you are now my brother in Christ.' From that day on we have lived and prayed and eaten meals with Jewish believers. I have committed my life, not to killing, but to saving as many lives as I can from the evil one. That is why I have given you this ride. I do it in the name of Jesus."

A sign posted the number of kilometers to Jerusalem. Judd could barely see the writing.

FOUR

Chang's Good News

As THE car neared the outskirts of Jerusalem, Judd saw the preparations for Nicolae's return. Banners and signs welcomed the potentate and all visitors. Trees and shrubbery had been planted to spruce up the city's appearance.

"What about the site of the earthquake?" Lionel said.

Sabir shook his head. "The 10 percent that was ravaged by the quake is still a disaster area. Some of the dead still haven't been found."

Judd hadn't seen this much excitement on the streets since the opening of the Gala before Nicolae's assassination. Overnight it seemed Carpathia had created jobs for hundreds of vendors selling trinkets and souvenirs. Some sold palm branches to wave at the potentate or lay in his path, a gesture of worship. Others peddled floppy hats, sandals, sunglasses, and even buttons with Nicolae's picture on the front. People could have their picture taken beside a life-size cutout of Carpathia, and one kiosk offered to record a person singing 'Hail Carpathia' and digitally add the person to the video from the day before in Tel Aviv.

Morale Monitors and Peacekeepers clogged streets with military vehicles. They were prepared for any kind of uprising.

Judd told Sabir the address for Sam and Mr. Stein, then called Chang. He expected to find Chang upset about Mac and the others, but Chang sounded upbeat.

"I'm sorry about what happened," Judd said. "Lionel and I were on the beach in Tel Aviv."

"I heard it came a lot closer to the spectators than it was supposed to," Chang said.

"Than it was supposed to? You mean they planned to crash?"

Chang chuckled. "I'm sorry. I forgot you didn't know."

"Know what?"

"Mac, David, Hannah, and Abdullah are fine. They weren't on the plane."

"Now I'm really confused," Judd said. "We

saw them fly over and do acrobatic stunts before the crash."

"Mac used a remote control to fly the plane. He had already programmed the craft to do those fancy maneuvers."

"But wouldn't he have to talk with people over the plane's radio?"

"Again, by remote control. They thought of everything."

Judd relayed the good news to Lionel and Sabir, and they both cheered. Judd asked, "But won't the GC know there was no one on the plane?"

"They intended to crash in the middle of the Mediterranean, but smashing on the beach was just as good. The GC haven't found any bodies and believe they must have been vaporized."

"But when they search their rooms, won't they be suspicious that all their stuff is gone?"

"That is the beauty of Ms. Palemoon's suggestion. She told them to pack like they were only going on a short trip. They left change on their dressers, and Mac even made a doctor's appointment for when he was scheduled to return."

"Perfect," Judd said.

"David scheduled staff meetings for next week as well. They even got into a fight with one of the cargo people about how much weight the plane was carrying. I'm sure they're blaming Mac or Director Hassid for overloading the aircraft. I'm telling you, no one suspects anything."

"So you're alone?"

"Yes, but I have much to keep me occupied. The Tribulation Force is converging on the Middle East, and it's my job to make sure Operation Eagle goes as planned."

"Back up. What are you talking about?"

"Because of what Dr. Ben-Judah believes is about to happen in Jerusalem, they have prepared for an evacuation. I will monitor the escape and stay tied in with the computers at the safe house in Illinois, keeping everyone up-to-date on how the mission is going."

"Who are they evacuating?"

"Anyone who wants to get away from Carpathia, but mostly the Jews and believers in Christ."

Chang told Judd the Tribulation Force's plans and how they had constructed a remote airstrip and refueling center right under the Global Community's nose in the Negev Desert. "They're going to airlift people there and then take them to Petra."

"Petra?" Judd said.

Chang's phone beeped. Judd wanted to hear more and ask Chang how he was coping with his dual marks, but Chang told Judd he would explain later.

Sabir slowed as they turned onto a familiar street. Judd told the story of meeting General Solomon Zimmerman at a meeting led by Mr. Stein. They passed Dr. Chaim Rosenzweig's estate, which had been burned to the ground.

Lionel gasped and pointed. General Zimmerman's home lay in charred ruins.

As Vicki and the others continued toward the Wisconsin hideout, she thought about the changes of the past few days. Her late-night discussion with Chad had helped her deal with her guilty feelings about Natalie's death. She still ached for the girl, but she knew Natalie would want her to keep going and helping as many as she could.

Thoughts of Natalie reminded Vicki of the e-mail that had caused such a stir among the kids. Vicki wanted to believe Claudia and talk with her about Natalie's last moments alive. Vicki pulled out a wrinkled copy of the e-mail and reread it.

> *Dear Young Tribulation Force,*
> *I need your help. My name is Claudia*

*Zander. I was Natalie Bishop's roommate.
Before she died, she talked with me about
God. I didn't want to listen at first, but now
that she's gone, I think what she said might
be true. She told me not to take the mark of
Carpathia, and I've only got a few more
days to comply. Please write back.
Claudia*

Vicki sighed and closed her eyes. She had
long ago decided to take every opportunity
to talk to others about God, no matter what
the risk. She had done a study of some of
the major characters in the Bible—from
Abraham to David to Jonah to Paul—and
discovered that God had taken them to
dangerous places.

Before she had become a believer, Vicki
took chances and lived on the edge. Now,
with so many bad things happening and the
Glorious Appearing a few years away, Vicki
felt more alive than ever. She believed God
had chosen to involve her in his great plan
and was calling *her* to dangerous places. At
times, that meant taking risks. Other times it
meant admitting she was wrong or revealing
her feelings to people around her. Deep
inside, Vicki ached to make a difference. She
saw people blindly following Carpathia and
hoping he had the answers.

She had written in her journal, *There is a spot in my heart God has touched that simply longs to follow. No matter where he sends me, no matter what he asks, I want to go.*

But as Vicki studied Claudia's note, something didn't feel right. The words felt calculated, like the girl had tried too hard to say the right thing or not to say the wrong thing. Dismissing Claudia's plea as a trick of the Global Community could be a mistake that would ruin Claudia's life for eternity. But meeting her face-to-face and falling for a trap would be equally wrong.

How do I know the right thing to do when the choices aren't clear? Vicki whispered. *How do I follow my heart when my heart doesn't know what to do?*

Vicki scribbled a note on a piece of paper. Before she was finished, she had scratched out words, written on the margins, and turned the paper over and started again.

> *Dear Claudia,*
>
> *Natalie mentioned you in some of our conversations. She said you were true-blue GC. I'm sorry to be hard on you, but I'm having trouble believing you would stop being faithful to Carpathia.*
>
> *If you want to know more about becom-*

*ing a believer, look on our Web site. You'll
find information and even a prayer. Whatever you do, don't take Carpathia's mark.
You'll regret it forever.*

Vicki showed the note to Conrad and
Shelly to get their input and the phone rang.

It was Darrion. "Melinda and I have tried
all the leads you gave, but we haven't been
able to find anything about Josey Fogarty.
We did come up with some pretty bad news
about her husband though."

"Tom?" Vicki said. "Did he die?"

"No," Darrion said. "He's working for the
Global Community."

Lionel walked to the front of General
Zimmerman's home. Judd had wanted to
keep moving, but Lionel felt a deep sadness
at seeing the beautiful house destroyed.

Judd shook his head. "The GC sure seems
to like starting fires to get rid of people."

Sabir joined them. "I would hate to think
someone found out about the band of
believers you have described."

"How can we find out if they survived?"
Judd said.

"What about Yitzhak?" Lionel said.

"Great idea," Judd said.

As they wove their way through the narrow streets to Yitzhak's home, Lionel explained how they had met the man and what he had done for them. He held his breath as they turned onto Yitzhak's street, afraid his home might have been torched as well. Lionel sighed when he saw it was still there.

Sabir followed Lionel and Judd up the front steps and Judd knocked on the door. Nothing. Judd knocked again and said, "Hello? Anybody home?"

"Just a moment," someone said. "Who is there?"

"Friends," Judd said.

A curtain opened and a man studied the three.

"We're looking for Yitzhak," Judd said. "Does he still live here?"

"What do you want with him?"

"We're friends."

The man opened the door and looked up and down the street. "Come in quickly."

Lionel followed Judd and Sabir into the home and the door closed behind them. "I see you have the mark of the believer. We have to be very careful. Global Community Morale Monitors have been active in this area."

Lionel couldn't believe the number of

people in the room when they reached the bottom of the stairs. They crowded so tightly that when Sam and Mr. Stein saw Judd and Lionel, it took them nearly a minute to move past the others to greet them.

"We have been praying for you since you left," Mr. Stein said as he hugged Judd. "I have just been going over our action plan for the next few days. Share what has happened to you since we last met."

"In front of everyone?" Judd said.

Mr. Stein smiled. "We are all anxious to hear."

Lionel held up both hands and smiled when Judd looked at him. "He asked you, not me."

Judd told the group what had happened with Z-Van in New Babylon. When he described Nicolae's funeral, everyone groaned. Judd asked Lionel to tell about Z-Van's pilot, Westin Jakes, and how he had prayed after Nicolae's resurrection. Several people said, "Praise God" and "Hallelujah," when Lionel finished.

Judd asked people to pray for their friend who was still working inside the Global Community and who had both the mark of the believer and Carpathia's mark.

The room fell silent. Then several people spoke up, not understanding how a person could have both marks. Judd tried to explain that his friend had been forced to take the mark of Carpathia against his will, but still the room grew louder.

Finally, Mr. Stein held up a hand and said it was time to end. After he led in prayer, people left in small groups through different doors so no one in the neighborhood would become suspicious.

Lionel moved to the back of the room as several people questioned Judd about the Global Community's plans in Israel. Sabir excused himself, hugged Lionel and Judd, and slipped into the night.

When the room was nearly empty, Mr. Stein took Judd and Lionel aside. "We have so much to tell you, so much to prepare you for, and so little time."

"What do you think will happen tomorrow?" Judd said.

"The evil one wants to defile the temple of God, but we are praying that it will actually bring people to the truth."

FIVE

The Enemy's Plans

VICKI reeled from the news that Tom Fogarty was now working for the Global Community. If Josey was a believer, how could the two live in the same house? Was Tom a secret believer behind enemy lines? Could Josey have died or moved away?

"What do you want me to do?" Darrion said.

"I need time to think. First, let me dictate a message to you that I've written to Natalie's roommate, Claudia." Vicki read the message and asked Darrion to send the response quickly.

"If it's a trap, she's probably going to ask for information about the group or to meet you," Darrion said.

"Exactly," Vicki said. "Let me call you back about the Fogartys."

Vicki spotted a sign welcoming travelers to Wisconsin. They only had a few hours of driving ahead, and she wanted to talk with Mark about the plan she was forming. She knelt on the floor by Mark's side and explained her idea about Cheryl and the baby going to live with Josey.

"Sounds complicated," Mark said. "If the husband is GC, you won't really know until you've talked with Josey."

"And we can't get in touch with her without going through her husband."

Colin held up a hand. "I have an idea. Pull over."

Mark found a rest area for travelers and pulled into the parking lot. The kids got out and stretched their legs as Vicki followed Colin inside.

Colin dialed information and got the number to the Global Community personnel department outside of Chicago. There he was told that Thomas Fogarty had been assigned to a new GC facility in Rockford, Illinois.

"That's not far from the Wisconsin line," Colin said, putting more money into the phone. He dialed the number for the Rockford station and asked to speak with Fogarty. "Do you know when he'll be back? . . . I see. Well, I have a friend who used to know him from his days in Chicago and wants to check in with him. Is there a good time to call back? . . . Okay. Oh, one more question. This is kind of awkward. Do you know if he and Josey are still together? . . . Right, I understand. Thanks a lot."

"What did they say?" Vicki said.

"She said she can't give out personal information."

Colin dialed another number and asked for a telephone listing for Thomas Fogarty in Rockford. He frowned and hung up. "Unlisted."

When they were back on the road, Jim Dekker phoned and asked about their progress. Colin told him where they were, and Jim said they shouldn't have any more trouble from the GC.

Vicki asked for the phone. "Jim, I hope you're getting out of there before they make you take the mark."

"I'm two steps ahead of you," Jim said. "I've packed everything I'll need for a few days and it's in my car. I'm hoping to see you guys in Wisconsin in a few hours."

Vicki gave him Tom Fogarty's name and asked if he could get a home number for him before he left.

"I'll do my best," Jim said.

Judd felt exhausted, and when he heard what was planned for the following day, he wanted to make sure he was rested. But when Sam and Mr. Stein began explaining what had happened since they had last seen them, and what they suspected from reading the Scriptures, Judd felt energized.

"First, we have to remember the truth about our enemy," Mr. Stein said. "Satan is much more powerful than any human, but he is still a created being. He will deceive many in the coming days and even scare people into following him, but we must remember that our God is still in control. He will only allow this pretender to continue his charade for a limited time."

"What does Carpathia have in mind this time?"

Sam started to speak, then stopped.

Mr. Stein smiled and waved a hand. "Go ahead."

"Well, Carpathia's true nature is about to be revealed," Sam said. "From the beginning of time, Satan has been against those whom God loved. He delighted in deceiving the man and woman in the Garden, and he has always been against God's chosen people, the Jews."

"But our God always has a plan," Mr. Stein

said, picking up the story. "He has a place of refuge for his people."

"Petra?"

Mr. Stein scratched his beard. "We do not know the exact place, but that is an interesting possibility."

Judd told them what he had heard from Chang. Sam became animated. "My father took me there when I was younger. It is one of the most unreachable places on earth."

"I've never heard of it," Lionel said.

"Petra is a city known for its red rock walls and its isolation," Sam said. "The only way to get inside is through the Siq, a mile-long path with cliffs on either side. There is a temple carved out of the rock 150 feet high. Inside the city are tombs and theaters and dwellings carved right out of the rock by ancient people. I think Petra would be a perfect place of refuge."

"Back up," Judd said. "As I understand it, Carpathia's going to defile the temple in some way and someone's going to stand up against him."

Mr. Stein nodded. "God has prepared the right person for the right time, but we have no idea who it will be."

"What about Tsion?" Judd said.

"Perhaps," Mr. Stein said. "We simply do not know."

"Well, it's clear from the reports that people in Jerusalem haven't been exactly anxious to put up a statue of Carpathia," Judd said.

Mr. Stein smiled. "Of course, believers would never want such a thing, but the Orthodox Jews and others have refused to even begin to build a replica statue. I believe the time is ripe for God to show his people the truth. Carpathia believes he is coming here to stamp out any opposition, but I believe God has something else in mind."

Sam sat forward. "We have heard some distressing things about Carpathia's schedule, so you must not be alarmed at what might happen. Don't be surprised if Carpathia does some sickening things."

"Like what?"

"Like mocking Jesus by walking down the Via Dolorosa, the same path of Christ's suffering just before his crucifixion."

"How are the Orthodox Jews and the Christ followers getting along?" Judd said.

"We are unified in our stand against Carpathia," Mr. Stein said. "On spiritual matters we are far apart. But I am trusting in the God who is able to open blind eyes. We pray they will see that Jesus is truly their Messiah."

Vicki couldn't wait to get to Colin's home and sleep. The kids had been on the run for so long that a long night's sleep was a luxury. For the past three and a half years, Vicki had learned to nap scrunched in a car, outside under the stars, or in some dark hideout. She longed to feel safe again, to have a place she could call her own, to simply sit and watch television without fear of being caught by the Global Community.

But the truth was, Vicki wouldn't trade her life now for what she had known before the disappearances. Her fears back then were that her parents would discover her sneaking out at night, or that she'd be grounded for flunking a class in school. A couple of her teachers had given her the line she always hated, "You have so much potential." Now, Vicki knew what they meant. If she studied and worked hard, God could use her to accomplish great things.

The phone rang and Colin handed it to her. "It's Jim."

Jim Dekker had escaped from the Global Community satellite operations center just before authorities came to apply the mark of Carpathia. "Before I left, I got an update on Pete in Iowa."

Vicki held her breath.

"He's still alive, and they're saying on the news that he's talking about Judah-ite groups around the country, that some young people have a hideout in Missouri. They're even saying he's talking about the location of Tsion Ben-Judah."

"Pete doesn't know where Tsion is. Nobody does."

"I know that, but reporters are saying Pete's spilling his guts about everything."

"Which means he's not giving them anything," Vicki said.

"You know they'll make him take the mark or choose the blade."

"Yeah. I know. Where are you?"

"Headed back to the house for a few things. As soon as they figure I've flown the coop, they'll come looking, and I don't want them to find my stash of uniforms and stuff. Should be a nice night for a bonfire. Too bad I can't stay around to roast marshmallows."

"Any luck with Mrs. Fogarty?"

"Almost forgot. I have the address and phone number right here."

Vicki repeated the address and phone number to make sure she had it right and told Jim to be careful. When she hung up, Colin turned and pointed to a map. "The address you mentioned is right across the state line, here. We're probably about fifteen to twenty minutes from there."

Vicki studied the map. "Should I call her?"

While Mr. Stein found a place for Judd to sleep, Lionel went with Sam. The boy seemed excited to have someone his age to talk with. "I want to show you what has angered so many."

Sam led Lionel to the familiar holy sites of the Old City. They passed the Wailing Wall where several Global Community guards stood watch. No one was allowed to worship or pray to anyone or anything other than Carpathia without permission.

When they neared the Temple Mount, Lionel heard construction and wondered who was still working at that time of night. They went around a corner and saw a huge staging area where the mark application would begin. It looked to Lionel like the staging area could hold several thousand. People would no doubt be herded toward the front, kept busy watching huge video screens.

"What are they going to play on that, a karaoke of 'Hail Carpathia'?" Lionel said.

Sam frowned. "Worse. Earlier I saw them

playing clips of Fortunato and Carpathia speeches. They show a segment with Fortunato calling fire down from heaven."

"I'll bet they have old Nicolae rising from the dead too."

"Of course," Sam said.

A few people had camped out by the crowd-control barriers to be first in line. When the monitors flickered and Carpathia came forth from his Plexiglas coffin on the huge screen, several cheered.

"So not all in Jerusalem are against Nicolae," Lionel said.

"Sadly, no. Mr. Stein says he believes some will be caught up in Carpathia's theatrics in the next few days and will be fooled or scared into taking his mark."

Lionel watched as a truck backed up to the area and unloaded a heavy box. Workers uncrated wooden parts and a sharp, metal object. Lionel realized it was a guillotine. "I've only seen pictures of them."

"Ugly, aren't they?"

Lionel shook his head. "What I can't believe is that people would willingly follow a man who would cut people's heads off simply because they believe in the true God."

Sam pawed at the dust with his foot. "I have a feeling this ground will be stained with the blood of some very brave people in the days to come."

A man walked toward them and Sam's face lit up. "Daniel!"

Daniel Yossef smiled and shook hands with Lionel as Sam introduced them. "I showed The Cube to Daniel three days ago and he still hasn't made up his mind."

Daniel smiled and nudged Lionel. "These young people come up with new ideas. I have to at least hear him out."

"What is holding you back from believing the truth?" Sam said.

Daniel waved a hand. "Let us not talk of things that divide us on this important night. Tomorrow your so-called evil ruler will visit. I have never seen him in person. If what you say about him is true, I will believe."

"Do not put off your decision," Sam said. "Carpathia deceives. It is his nature to—"

"You told me yourself that you cannot make this decision for me. Do you see a mark on my forehead or my hand? Let me investigate what you have said, see the man in action, and decide."

Sam shook his head. "I do not know what else you need to see. He has come against the people of God."

"He signed a treaty of peace, but you

Judah-ites won't stop accusing him." Daniel smiled and patted Sam on the back. "Let me do this my way. If you're right, I'll be the first to admit it."

"All right," Sam said. "I will be praying for you."

As Sam and Lionel walked back to Yitzhak's house, Sam talked about Daniel and how they had met only three days earlier. "Perhaps it's that he looks so much like my father, but I have a deep concern for the man."

"Has Mr. Stein talked to him?" Lionel said.

"No. I hope to get them together soon."

"How are you coping with your father's death?"

Sam sighed. "Sometimes I wonder what would have happened if I had tried to explain my faith in some other way. I picture my father and I telling others the truth about God, speaking to anyone who will listen. But that is only a dream."

Sam put a hand on Lionel's shoulder. "Reality is that I now have a heavenly Father and brothers and sisters in the faith who care about me."

Vicki's hands shook as she dialed Josey Fogarty's home phone. She wondered what would happen if Tom answered. Were they

making a mistake to bring Josey into their
problem?

After four rings, the answering machine
picked up. Tom's gruff voice said, "You've
reached the Fogartys. As you can tell, we're
not able to answer your call. Leave a
message. He is risen."

The last phrase startled Vicki for a moment
and she realized her stuttering was being
recorded. "Uh, Josey? I don't know if you'll
remember me or not, but I really need to
talk. I'll try back in about—"

The phone picked up and a woman said,
"Hello? Who is this?"

"Is this Josey?" Vicki managed.

Vicki could tell the woman had been
crying. "Yes, it's me. Go ahead and come for
me. I don't care anymore."

"I don't understand—," Vicki said.

"Yes, you do. Well, I don't care what you
do to me!"

"Josey, it's Vicki Byrne."

The woman sniffed and caught her breath.
"Vicki? I don't believe it."

"I'm only a few minutes from your house.
Do you mind if I come see you?"

The woman sobbed. Finally she said, "Yes,
I would love to see you again."

SIX

Finding Josey

IT WAS after midnight when Lionel found a place to sleep. He was grateful that God had led them to Yitzhak's house and that they had reconnected with their friends. Before Sam left, Lionel asked about General Zimmerman, the man who had opened his home up to so many believers.

Sam looked at the floor and whispered, "We were speaking openly in the streets with some of the undecided when a band of Global Community officers approached and asked the General to follow them. He looked at us, not knowing what to do. Finally, when he saw things might get violent if he refused, he went with them.

"Mr. Stein and I came here to begin a time of intense prayer. The next night, one of the

General's servants who had become a believer rushed to tell us that the GC had surrounded his home. We believe everyone got out before they set it on fire."

Lionel shook his head. "Have you heard anything from him since?"

Sam nodded. "We continued to pray that God would protect him and have him released. However, when the GC began marking their prisoners, the newspaper carried the story of General Zimmerman's choice of the blade."

Lionel bit his lip. "You know, we were responsible for putting him in that situation."

Sam smiled. "You and the others helped him see the truth, and today, though it pains us to lose him in such a terrible way, he is with God."

Lionel went to bed with thoughts of Carpathia and what would happen the next day. Would he and Judd be treated the same way as General Zimmerman? As Lionel fell asleep, he was praying for Vicki and his friends back home.

As they drove closer to Josey's home, Vicki studied the countryside west of Rockford.

Some areas still showed the effects of the great earthquake. Trees and grass had been scorched by the plague of fire, and residents had done their best to try and bring back some of the beauty of the city.

Mark continued his protest of the plan, though he admitted some curiosity about seeing Josey and finding out what had happened to her. He had talked with Judd many times about the sting operation against Cornelius Grey and LeRoy Banks, two bad guys the kids had helped catch. Mark's main concern was that they not be anywhere near Global Community officers who were sure to be on alert.

Vicki felt a tingle down her spine as they came closer. She had often thought of Josey and hoped to one day meet again.

"Turn left here," Colin said.

Josey's street seemed similar to Judd's in Mount Prospect. The houses were nice, with big, fenced-in backyards, but the place seemed deserted. *All this space and no children*, Vicki thought.

Mark drove past the house and turned around, making sure everything looked okay. He parked on the street and the kids unbuckled.

"Let Vicki go first and talk with Mrs.

Fogarty," Colin said. Everyone agreed and Colin gave Vicki one of the handheld radios from their operation in Iowa. "If anything goes wrong, call us. We'll be waiting."

Josey opened the door before Vicki could knock. Vicki recalled first meeting the woman and being blown away by her simple beauty. Though Josey didn't wear makeup, not even lipstick, her pale blue eyes, sandy blonde hair, trim figure, and huge, easy smile were striking. Now, only three years later, Josey appeared to have aged ten years. Her hair was tinged with gray, her face, cutely freckled before, was wrinkled. Her eyes were bloodshot and puffy. The woman was still trim, and Vicki couldn't help thinking she looked gaunt.

"Come in, Vicki," Josey said in her familiar husky voice.

Vicki hugged her. "It's been a long time."

"Too long. Are you with friends?"

Vicki nodded. "They thought it would be best for us to talk alone first."

Josey showed her into the living room and brought her a hot cup of tea. She wiped away a tear and sat next to Vicki. Vicki wanted to tell her everything, but she sensed the woman needed to talk.

"I need to ask first about your husband," Vicki said quietly.

"I understand. He's not a believer, if that's what you mean."

Vicki scooted forward. "And he works for the Global Community?"

Josey nodded.

"Has he taken Carpathia's mark?"

Josey sighed. "The Global Community came in and took over. If he was going to stay in law enforcement, he had to go with them."

Vicki put a hand on her arm. "I need to know if he's taken the mark."

Josey hung her head and sighed. "Not yet. But with all that's going on around the country, this new commander, Fulcire, is pressuring employees to take it quickly."

Vicki took the woman by the shoulders. "You have to convince him not to take it."

"He'd have to leave the GC."

"Exactly."

"He's not going to do that."

Vicki asked more questions, but the woman broke down. When she stopped crying, Vicki asked what had happened after they last saw each other.

"Tom went back to work and pushed God aside. I started reading the Bible and studying, trying to understand what would happen next. I didn't want to beat Tom over the head with my beliefs, so I was careful to not come on too strong. But at times, I couldn't help it. I'd find a passage that really helped, and I'd want to share it."

"Did it drive him away?"

"At first he thought it was just a phase I was going through," Josey said. "I'd been into crystals, channeling, astrology, and angels. You name it, I'd tried it. I'd hop from one to another as fast as some people switch channels on their TV. I think he figured my belief in Jesus would change sooner or later too."

"But it didn't?"

For the first time since Vicki walked in, Josey showed a hint of a smile. "I can't say that I've been perfect in following him, but I still believe in God. It's just that I've had no one to talk with. The first time I saw someone with the mark of the believer, I nearly fainted."

"We're going to have to get you plugged into an on-line group."

"I didn't want to offend Tom, and I know how much the GC hate underground groups, so I backed off. Then the earthquake came and we moved here and I've been sort of stagnant."

"What happened when the locusts came?"

"Tom was stung the first day and suffered for months. He couldn't believe they didn't sting me, and I told him it was because I was protected by God. He wouldn't listen."

"So you've seen no change in him?"

"At times he seems open. I even saw him cry once when I started talking about my boys, but most of the time he just seems mad at God."

"And you've been alone, so it's been hard to grow."

Josey nodded. "I've read your Web site, and Tsion's of course, but I've been so worried about Tom that I'm afraid I haven't been much good to the cause."

"Don't say that," Vicki said. "God gives everybody a gift and—"

"That's why I feel so guilty. I could be doing something, using my hospitality to have people in and tell them the truth, but here I sit, paralyzed with fear that my husband is going to come home with the mark of Carpathia on his forehead and ask me to do the same. That's who I thought you were on the phone, the GC coming to take me away."

"You don't have to worry about taking the mark," Vicki said. "God will give you the strength to resist it."

Josey wiped her eyes. Vicki didn't want to bring up Cheryl's situation until the time was right.

"Do you think there's still hope for Tom?" Josey said.

"I have to admit, if he's known the truth this long and has still waited—"

"He sees through Carpathia," Josey interrupted. "He knows the guy isn't what he seems."

"Then why is he working for the GC?"

Josey shook her head.

"Does he know that you won't take the mark?"

"We've talked about it. He says he'll keep my secret, and no one needs to know, but I'm scared."

"You should be." Vicki looked at her watch and keyed the microphone on the walkie-talkie. "Mark, where are you?"

"End of the street. You want us to come?"

Someone moved behind Vicki, and Josey put a hand to her mouth and gasped. Vicki turned and saw Tom Fogarty staring at her.

"How long have you been here, hon?" Josey said.

"Vicki, you want us to come over there?" Mark said.

"No, stay where you are," Vicki said, returning Fogarty's stare.

"So, Vicki Byrne, Vicki B., Jackie Browne, or whoever you're calling yourself these days," Tom said, "I've been following your little rebellion against the Global Community."

"Tom, Vicki was one of the kids who helped you—"

"I know what she did, and I know her friends on the other end of that radio are probably the ones wanted in Iowa. Am I right?"

Vicki stared at the man and stayed silent. She had wanted to help Cheryl so much that she hadn't counted on this. Now she was trapped.

"You just going to sit there, or are you going to try and save my soul too?" Tom said.

"Vicki, is something wrong in there?" Mark said on the walkie-talkie. "Conrad said he thought he saw someone walk through the backyard a moment ago."

Vicki keyed the microphone. "Just stay where you are. I'm okay for now."

"Why don't you tell your friends I can have ten squad cars and a couple of choppers here in five minutes?" Tom said.

"Tom, you won't," Josey said.

"You don't know what this girl and her friends have been up to. Stealing satellite trucks. Breaking into international video hookups. I was there at that schoolhouse after you kids left."

"Did you burn it down?" Vicki said coolly.

"Whatever she's done, it's been for a good reason," Josey said.

"Ends justify the means, huh? I thought Jesus followers were supposed to be good, law-abiding citizens. Instead, you break people out of jail and defy every rule the Global Community has made."

As she listened, Vicki thought about the others in the van. Fogarty could have already called in a team of GC officers before he walked into the room. She stood and faced him. "You used to be a cop, and a good one from what Judd told me. You shot straight with people, even perps, and they respected you."

Fogarty pursed his lips and lifted his hands. "What's your point?"

"Well, I'll shoot straight with you. I assume since you're telling me all this that you haven't talked about me and my friends to your superiors. You've been following us on your own, wondering when we'd make a mistake."

"Keep going."

"And if you're willing to keep quiet about us, there must be some reason. You must agree with what we're doing, or at least are willing to look the other way."

"I feel sorry for people who are misguided, that's all."

"Well, here's the story. I met this girl in Iowa. She's pregnant. Two, maybe three months along. She's had a hard life and the baby will have an even harder time if I don't do something about it."

Vicki looked at Josey. "I was thinking about her situation, and for some reason the names of your two boys popped into my head. I don't know why."

Josey put a hand over her mouth and shook. Tom's mouth dropped as he sat on the edge of a chair.

"She's not prepared to care for a child, and I asked how she would feel if we found someone to adopt it. Maybe take care of her while she was having it. Someone with experience."

"What did she say?" Josey said, her eyes wide and filled with tears.

"She wants the baby to have the right family. That's why I'm here."

"Praise God," Josey said, and she broke down. Tom fell back onto the chair and stared at the ceiling.

Vicki knew something was going on with Tom and Josey, but she didn't know what.

Finally, Josey spoke. "I didn't tell you this, Vicki, but the doctors told me I would never

have children again. A few weeks ago Tom
and I were talking and I was trying to tell
him how good God is, that he wants to help
us. Tom brought up Ben and Brad—he
always loved them even though they didn't
live with us—and said God was selfish and
mean to take them."

Josey fought the tears. "I asked what it
would take to get him to believe God was
there and wanted a relationship."

Vicki looked at Tom. "What did you say?"

Tom Fogarty, former Chicago policeman
and now Global Community tough guy,
shook in his chair, overcome with emotion.
When he could finally speak he said, "I told
her . . . I would believe in God . . . when he
gave us a baby."

SEVEN

Fogarty's Dilemma

Vicki didn't know what to say or do, other than put an arm around Josey and hug her.

Tom had moved to the window and stared out at the street. "Your friends out there?"

Vicki nodded. "What are you going to do?"

"I'd be the GC hero of the day if I brought you guys in."

"But you're not going to?"

Tom turned. "In the morning everyone will be talking about Carpathia and what a great god he is."

"And you?"

Tom shook his head.

Josey reached for him and said, "This is a perfect time to give your life to the true God. You know everything I've been telling you is true. And our prayers have been answered."

Tom looked at Vicki. "You think this girl

would let us care for the baby if I'm working for the GC?"

"I think that puts her and Josey in too much danger," Vicki said.

"So you think I'm going to just give in and get religion?"

Josey said, "It's not religion—"

"I know, it's a relationship. I've heard that about a million times." Tom paced in front of the window, gesturing wildly. "I've lived my entire life without God. I've never tried to use religion as a crutch—"

"And you think that's what *we're* doing?" Josey said.

"I didn't say that—"

"It takes a lot bigger man to admit he needs help than one who says he can do it himself," Josey said. "You've arrested enough people in your career who have done it their own way and paid the price."

"I'm not going to say I believe this just to make you guys happy, or to make sure we get that baby."

"I'm glad," Josey said, "because we'd know you were faking it."

Tom rolled his eyes. "Oh yeah, the thing on the forehead."

Vicki stepped forward. "Mr. Fogarty, the Bible talks about people being blinded to the truth at this time of history. I don't know how it works, but it's clear there's something supernatural going on that keeps people from believing what's obvious."

"So I've been blinded by little demons running around? Or maybe by Satan himself? You expect me to buy that?"

Vicki put out her hand to stop him from pacing. "I'm not asking that you buy anything. Just stop and ask God to take the blinders off. If he's real, he'll help you understand the truth. Are you willing?"

Tom stopped and folded his arms. "All right, but I feel stupid."

"It's okay," Vicki said. "You want me to pray with you?"

"No, I can handle it." Tom cleared his throat and took a deep breath. "God, I know that my wife and this girl care about me, and they've said if I pray, you'll open my eyes. So if you're there, I pray you'd show me where I'm wrong and what I need to do about it. Amen."

The radio crackled with Mark's voice. "Vicki, we need some direction here. There's a car pulling up to the house."

Tom pulled the curtain back, looked out the window, and cursed. "It's my partner. Tell your guys to get out of the neighborhood. Vicki, you go upstairs with Josey."

"Is this a trap?" Vicki said.

Tom scowled. "Just go upstairs. He's coming up the sidewalk."

As she followed Josey upstairs, Vicki told Mark she needed more time. "We've got GC company, so move the van out of sight and maintain silence until I get back to you."

Josey left the door open a crack as Tom's partner knocked downstairs. Vicki strained to hear as the men laughed and walked into the kitchen.

"His partner's name is Cal Trachsel. They've been together since we moved here."

"Is Cal 100 percent GC?"

Josey shook her head and closed the door. "I think he knows there are problems just like Tom. He's pretty levelheaded."

"Have you ever talked to him about God?"

"No. I've only met him face-to-face twice. He calls for Tom a lot and we chat, but that's about it."

The front door closed and Josey walked to the stairs. "Tom?"

When he didn't answer, Josey went to the window and made sure Cal was leaving. Vicki followed the woman downstairs to the kitchen and found Tom sitting at the table, his head in his hands.

"What's the matter?" Josey said.

"That's the first time I've ever lied to my

partner. A relationship like that is built on trust. Now I've violated it."

"What did he want?" Josey said.

"He wanted to make sure I was okay, and that I understood what would happen if I didn't comply."

"Comply with what?"

"His new tattoo. He got it on the back of his hand."

"Oh no," Vicki said.

"Memo came down saying we had to take the mark this afternoon."

"Is that why you came here?"

"I felt a little conflicted, yes. My wife tells me I'll be selling my soul and flushing my eternal existence if I do this, and the Global Community tells me they'll chop my head off if I don't comply."

"What did you tell Cal?"

Vicki felt like an intruder on the conversation, but she stood in the background and listened.

Tom's face twisted and turned red the more he talked about his situation. "I told him you haven't been feeling well and I wanted to make sure you were all right."

"Why did you lie?"

Tom stood and pushed his chair back. "Maybe I was scared of losing you. Maybe I was scared of losing myself, and I came back here to . . ."

"To what?" Vicki said.

Josey sat forward. "You don't want to take that mark, do you?"

"I don't know," Tom said, running a hand through his hair. "I had it all planned. I was going to convince you to take the mark and we'd be okay. I figured you'd leave this Christian thing behind, but it's clear you're serious."

Vicki went to the living room and found Josey's computer. As she logged on to www.theunderground-online.com, Vicki contacted Mark and briefly explained the situation.

"Would it help if Colin talked to Mr. Fogarty?" Mark said.

"Give him a few more minutes," Vicki said. "But be ready."

"Vicki, we need to get moving," Colin said.

"Just a few more minutes."

Vicki noticed an e-mail from Claudia, but she didn't dare open it at such a critical time. A war was raging in Tom's mind, and the only question now was who would win, the true God or Nicolae? Vicki asked to see Tom in the living room.

"One of the things we wanted to do with

our Web site was lay out the truth of the Bible so anyone could understand it."

"I've seen this," Tom said. "We read your Web site and Tsion Ben-Judah's to look for clues."

"But you haven't looked at it since you asked God to open your eyes, right?"

Tom nodded and sat. Vicki pulled up different Old Testament prophecies that pointed to Jesus Christ. As she explained, she noticed Tom trying to concentrate, rubbing his forehead, and perspiring.

"I understand what you're saying," Tom said when Vicki was through. "I understood it when Josey explained it a long time ago. I'm just not sure I can believe in something just because it gets me to heaven. I don't want to face any more of the judgments you talk about, but I don't want you to scare me into a decision."

"The point isn't escaping judgments or not getting stung by some evil creature, it's choosing to follow the true God. You have to decide whether you're going to follow the one who gave his life to save you, or the one who threatens to cut off your head if you don't follow him."

Tom scratched his head. "I hadn't thought about it that way."

Vicki pulled up an Old Testament verse Tsion Ben-Judah had used on his Web site. "At a crucial time for Israel," she said, "a leader named Joshua challenged people to follow the true God instead of the fake ones they had worshiped. He wanted to make sure they understood how important their decision was."

Tom read the verse aloud. " 'So honor the Lord and serve him wholeheartedly. . . . But if you are unwilling to serve the Lord, then choose today whom you will serve. . . . But as for me and my family, we will serve the Lord.' "

Vicki prayed silently. She had given Tom the truth, backing up her beliefs with the Bible. Josey had lived the truth before him the past few years. Now it was Tom's decision.

The phone rang and Josey looked at the caller ID. "It's from work."

When it stopped ringing, Tom took a breath. "So what happens if I decide like you want me to? We go on the run? Try to hide for the rest of our lives?"

"Honey, if you choose him, God will take care of us."

Tom nodded. "I asked him to take off the blinders. I can see this is the only sane decision I can make, but I feel like I'm choosing more *against* Carpathia than *for* God."

A car pulled up in front of the house. Josey ran to the window and gasped. "It's a GC squad car."

"Cal said they're sending officers to pick up off-duty people to give the mark."

"No," Josey said, "tell them you're not going."

A car door slammed.

"You need to pray," Vicki said. "Just ask God to forgive—"

"I have to stall them. Josey, pack some things."

"Don't put this off," Vicki pleaded.

Someone knocked on the door.

Tom lowered his voice. "Do your people have enough room for two more in their van?"

"We'll make room," Vicki whispered.

"Go upstairs, get on your radio, and have your people drive to the end of the cul-de-sac—"

Thump, thump. "Officer Fogarty? Global Community Peacekeeper. Open up, please."

"Don't let them go down this street," Fogarty said. "Have them park on the next street, just west of us, in the same part of the block."

Vicki sprinted to a room at the top of the stairs. She pushed the door almost closed as

Tom opened the front door. Out of breath, Vicki listened to the man outside.

"Officer Fogarty, we've been instructed to bring all Global Community personnel to the station for the loyalty mark application."

"Yeah, I know. I was headed back that way as soon as I checked my wife. I told my partner she's not feeling well—"

"You'll need to come with me, sir."

From the next room came a shriek and a sob that sent chills down Vicki's spine. "Tom, I need you!" Josey wailed. "Hurry!"

Vicki peeked through the crack in the door. As Tom started toward the stairs, the officer grabbed Fogarty's arm. "I'm sorry, sir. I have orders."

"And I have a wife in pain! Surely the Global Community has enough compassion to let a man comfort his wife."

"Your wife can come with us if she—"

Josey wailed again and Tom shook free of the man. "She's in no condition to be moved." He pushed past the officer and ran upstairs.

"I'll give you five minutes," the officer said, stepping outside.

Vicki pressed the Talk button of the walkie-talkie and whispered instructions for Mark. Mark clicked his radio twice, the signal that they had heard and were on their way.

Vicki joined Tom and Josey in the next room and quietly locked the door. Tom had the window open and a duffel bag filled with clothes lay on the bed. He threw the bag out the window, and Josey climbed onto the lattice that ran to the bottom of the wall.

"Quickly," Tom whispered.

As Josey carefully climbed down, Vicki helped push a dresser in front of the door. Then Tom helped her through the window and onto the lattice. It felt rickety, and Vicki wondered if it would hold her weight.

When she was almost to the bottom, a voice yelled from inside the house. "Officer Fogarty, it's time. Come down immediately or I'll come up there and get you."

EIGHT

Tom's Decision

VICKI and Josey hopped over a fence and ran between two houses toward the next street. Vicki glanced behind them as Tom dropped to the ground and picked up the duffel bag.

Vicki spotted the van about three houses away. She put a hand to the front gate when Tom whispered, "Get down!"

Vicki fell behind a bush, breathing hard. She glanced at the Fogartys' house and saw the GC officer at a window. "The window's open and I think he's making a run for it, sir!" the officer said into his radio. When he moved away, Tom raced forward.

"I see him now, sir," the officer said. "He's running toward the next street. I'm giving chase."

Vicki opened the gate and waved wildly at Mark. The van pulled forward and Vicki, Josey, and Tom jumped in as Mark floored the accelerator. Colin grabbed the duffel bag as Tom struggled to get the door closed.

"Take a right at the stop sign," Tom said.

"Was that officer alone?" Josey said.

"I think so, and he followed us on foot, so we've got a chance."

Mark turned right and Tom directed him to an unpaved road that cut across a field. A few minutes later, with Tom's help, they were headed north to the Wisconsin border.

Josey stared out the window, holding a scrape on her arm from the lattice. "I can't believe we've just left everything behind. I only had a few minutes to decide what to take and what to leave."

Mark glanced at Tom, then glared at Vicki in the rearview mirror. "What were you thinking?" he mouthed.

Vicki put a finger to her lips. She introduced Mark and Colin, then turned to Shelly and Conrad. Finally, Cheryl leaned forward and held Josey's hand. "I'm very glad to meet you, ma'am."

Josey teared up, turned in the seat, and hugged the girl. "And I'm glad to meet you."

Tom listened to his GC radio and

watched for any activity. When they reached the Wisconsin border, he seemed to relax.

"What would they have done with you if you stayed?" Mark said.

"I guess they would have made me choose. Everybody was required to take the mark at some point today."

"And why didn't you?" Mark said.

Tom sighed. "The truth is, I've been having second thoughts all along. I didn't want my wife to know it, but the whole GC system was bugging me. I kept hoping things would get better, but they didn't."

"So you want to pray now?" Vicki said.

Tom looked around the car at the others. "I guess this is as good a place as any." He put his hands together and leaned forward against the back of the seat in front of him.

Josey put a hand on his back and asked if he needed help. He nodded. "Just tell God that you're sorry about your sin and that you want to receive his forgiveness. You believe that Jesus died on the cross and paid the penalty for what you've done. You also believe that God raised Jesus from the dead and wants to give that new life to you. You receive his gift right now, and you want him to guide your life from this day on."

Tom nodded again and began. To Vicki's surprise, he prayed aloud. "God, you know what a mess I've made of my life and how long I've rejected you. I've done some bad things, things even Josey doesn't know about. So I'm asking you right now to forgive me. I want to receive that gift you're offering. I do believe you died for me, and that you rose from the dead. Give me a new life, and change me."

"Amen," Josey said softly.

When Tom looked up, Josey touched his face and smiled. Tom looked at her, then at Vicki and the others in astonishment. "I don't believe it. You guys were serious about God giving you a mark."

After everyone had congratulated Tom, Josey pulled out a tattered photo album from the duffel bag. "When you have to pack in five minutes, you realize what's most important."

Josey flipped through pages of photos, memories, ticket stubs, and important events. She showed Vicki the last pictures she had taken of her two boys, Ben and Brad, before the disappearances.

Mark turned the van east, toward the kids' new hideout, with a brand-new believer, Tom Fogarty.

Judd awoke early after a good night's sleep and joined the others in the basement for breakfast. Lionel had come in late, so Judd tried to keep quiet and let him sleep.

Yitzhak and Mr. Stein were leading the others in prayer for the events of the day. Though Mr. Stein said he knew what Nicolae's ultimate plan was, he confessed he did not know exactly how things would take place.

"You must remember that Nicolae wants to set himself up as a divine being. He is intent on the destruction of all of God's creation, both human and otherwise. From my reading of Scripture, his persecution of the Jewish people will begin soon."

"Many people do not want to take Carpathia's mark," one man said, "but they do not believe that Jesus is the Messiah. How can we persuade them?"

Mr. Stein nodded. "We must continue to pray that God will reveal himself and convince them. The fact that they do not recognize Carpathia as a god is very encouraging. But simply seeing the truth about evil is not enough. They must believe the truth about Jesus."

Though Judd knew what would happen would probably disgust him, he still felt a sense of excitement about the day and prayed God would protect him. He prayed for the others in the Young Trib Force and decided to check with Chang before he left.

Chang answered the phone and explained that he was at his computer in the palace, monitoring the complex number of pilots, planes, drivers, and vehicles that would help with the mass departure of people from Jerusalem.

"I still don't understand how they're going to slip by the GC," Judd said.

"As long as the GC believes what the Trib Force is doing is one of their own exercises, Operation Eagle will continue."

"How did they come up with that name?"

"It comes from a passage in Revelation 12. 'She was given two wings like those of a great eagle. This allowed her to fly to a place prepared for her in the wilderness, where she would be cared for and protected from the dragon for a time, times, and half a time.' Tsion believes the woman represents God's chosen people. The two wings are land and air, and her place is Petra."

"How long are people supposed to stay there?"

"Dr. Ben-Judah teaches that 'a time' is one

year, so 'a time, times, and half a time' would be three and a half years of protection."

"And the serpent is Nicolae?"

"Yes, Antichrist."

"Any news about the GC finding anything in the plane crash?"

"They are still combing the wreckage. The four are presumed dead, but there's no final report."

Something in Chang's voice bothered Judd and he asked if the boy was all right. When Chang paused, Judd said, "I know you're under a lot of pressure, but I might be able to help."

"I have talked with Dr. Ben-Judah this morning about . . . my problem."

"The dual marks?"

"Yes. He understands how alone I feel, and he tried to help me, but I still can't look in the mirror. This mark of Carpathia mocks me."

"What did Tsion say?"

"He assured me that I have the seal of God and that I did not voluntarily receive the mark. But in Dr. Ben-Judah's own writings, he says the mark of the beast condemns me."

"The Bible says you can't *take* both marks. You didn't *take* it—they forced it on you."

"Which is exactly what he said. But I keep

thinking about the brave ones who stayed faithful to the end. God gave them the ability to face the blade without fear. What did I do?"

"You've stayed in the den of the lion," Judd said. "Don't tell me you're chicken. You're in the most dangerous place on the face of the earth."

Chang was silent a moment. "I appreciate you trying to encourage me, but even Dr. Ben-Judah admits my problem puzzles him. The only thing I can do is stay at my post and fulfill my duties until he contacts me again."

Vicki and the others were given a hero's welcome when they arrived safely in Wisconsin. Becky Dial greeted her husband warmly, and Phoenix went wild when he saw Vicki. Charlie had to put him in another room so they could hear the story of what happened.

Janie hugged Vicki and told her she'd been praying for her. The kids all welcomed Josey and Tom Fogarty, but with all of the new people added, Vicki wondered if there would be enough room.

Darrion pulled Vicki aside a few minutes after she arrived. "I know you have to be tired, but I'd like you to look at Claudia's response."

Vicki nodded. "I saw that she'd written, but I haven't had time to look at it."

Darrion pulled up the response, which had Vicki's message pasted at the front of the e-mail. Claudia wrote underneath:

> *Dear Young Trib Force,*
>
> *I totally understand how you might think this is a trap. You probably get that a lot. I have visited your Web site many times and I decided to pray the prayer, but nothing happened. I don't see a mark on my fore-head or on anyone else's. We only have another day to comply with taking Carpathia's mark. What should I do?*
> *Claudia*

Vicki took a breath and sighed. "It's not what I expected."

"What did you think she'd do, write some nasty note admitting she was a Carpathia follower?" Darrion said.

Vicki looked hard at Darrion. "What if she's telling the truth? What if she's really a believer and we just let her hang down there? I thought she'd ask for a face-to-face meeting, but she didn't."

"If she's a true believer, don't you think she'd have the sense to get out?"

Vicki squeezed her forehead with a hand and pulled her hair back. "I'm too tired to think straight."

"Then do this," Darrion said. "Write her back and tell her to get out of there as fast as she can. When she's a safe distance away, write us again and we'll try to help."

"Sounds good."

While Darrion worked on the return e-mail, Vicki talked with Jim Dekker and the other new arrivals. Ginny and Bo Shairton nearly cried when they saw Vicki, and Maggie Carlson wept as she talked about Natalie's sacrifice for them.

Vicki found Manny Aguilara a shy young man, with multiple tattoos on his neck and arms. He said he felt out of place but very welcomed.

"I would like to tell you my story when you are rested," Manny said.

"I'd love to hear it," Vicki said.

Vicki found a cot in one of the girls' rooms and listened to the conversation through the thin walls. Tom Fogarty asked questions, Josey talked with Charlie about his family, and Shelly told Janie and Melinda about Chad Harris, the good-looking guy they had met in Iowa.

When she was almost asleep, Vicki was startled by something moving against her cot. She leaned over and saw Phoenix wagging his tail. She patted the covers and the dog jumped onto the cot and slept at her feet the entire night.

The sun was coming up as Judd finished talking with Chang. Judd told him he would be praying for him throughout the day.

"Thank you," Chang said, "but don't forget to pray for Dr. Rosenzweig as well."

"Where is he?"

"You don't know? Dr. Rosenzweig is the one who will stand up to Carpathia."

"What?" Judd said. "I thought it was going to be Tsion."

"Dr. Rosenzweig has been studying with Dr. Ben-Judah, and for some reason he is going to be the main person to challenge Nicolae."

Judd thought it through. Chaim was Jewish, a believer in Jesus as Messiah, but he didn't fit the profile of a prophet. He had heard the man speak before, and his voice wasn't strong and commanding like Tsion's had been. Still, if Chaim was God's chosen, God could give him the strength he needed.

Judd told Chang he would check with him later and he went to wake Lionel. This was going to be a day no one alive would forget.

NINE

The Gathering Storm

JUDD met with Lionel and Sam and discovered from one of the Jewish believers that Carpathia was supposed to appear in the Old City at 11 A.M.

"That will give me time to show you some of what's happened since you left," Sam said.

Sam showed them several meeting places used since the fire at General Zimmerman's home. A few were secluded, where people could secretly ask questions without fear of Global Community crackdown. Others were out in the open.

"And the GC never stopped you or arrested you?" Lionel said.

"A few people have been arrested," Sam said, "but God has protected us and allowed us to talk with hundreds. Plus, we've been using this." Sam pulled out a handheld

computer and activated the screen, showing
The Cube, a high-tech presentation of the
gospel.

"I hope we get to meet the guy who devel-
oped that someday," Lionel said.

Sam took them through a major street as
they moved toward the Old City. People
swarmed out of hotels looking for transportation. Lionel nudged Judd and pointed at a
convoy of Global Community troops. "I
thought this guy was for peace. Are those just
toy guns and missiles?"

Judd shook his head. Convoys of tanks,
fighters, and bombers rolled by, and people
cheered when they saw the show of military
might.

They reached the Via Dolorosa before 9
A.M. and were surrounded by masses looking
for a spot to view Carpathia. Judd's parents
had taken him to parades in Chicago and the
suburbs, but they were nothing like this. Men
and women elbowed their way to the best
spots. Global Community Peacekeepers and
Morale Monitors moved through the crowds
in small groups.

GC sharpshooters prowled tops of
buildings. It was clear this event would not
be marred by another assassination
attempt.

Vendors had run out of real palm

branches, so they sold plastic ones to toss before the potentate. People who supported Carpathia talked about his "triumphal entry" and Judd could hardly stand it. Hawkers walked up and down the streets selling paintings of Nicolae coming back to life, pictures of Carpathia standing on his glass coffin, and even commemorative coins featuring numbers from the different regions of the world. Judd couldn't believe that one man was selling replicas of guillotines. He called them "Judah-ite Eliminators" and had sold hundreds.

Sam pointed out many who were Orthodox Jews. These men scowled and sneered at the vendors.

There were fewer Peacekeepers and Morale Monitors inside the Old City. Some shop-windows and businesses were boarded up, still feeling the effects of the Jerusalem earthquake. A man with a handheld television near Judd called for quiet as Reverend Father Leon Fortunato's face appeared on a newscast. The news anchor spoke of Fortunato in glowing terms, saying the man was bringing the world together through his efforts to bring peace and healing to a hurting world.

Lionel rolled his eyes as the news showed yet another replay of the airplane crash in Tel

Aviv. Security and Intelligence Director Suhail Akbar appeared at a press conference held earlier that morning.

"Unfortunately," Akbar said, "while the investigation continues, we have been unable to confirm the evidence of any human remains. It is, of course, possible that four loyal patriots of the Global Community were vaporized upon impact in this tragedy. Medical personnel tell us they would have died without pain. Once we have confirmed the deaths, prayers will go to the risen potentate on behalf of their eternal souls, and we will extend our sympathies to their families and loved ones."

"We have learned from sources inside the investigation," the news anchor said, "that the crash may have been caused by pilot error. GCNN has learned that the flight crew was warned before takeoff of a cargo weight-and-balance problem. We'll have more on that story as it develops."

"Sounds like the GC took the bait," Lionel whispered to Judd.

"Let's hope they don't catch on."

Judd's phone blipped and it was Chang. He asked where Judd was and Judd told him.

"I have big news. Mr. Hassid just had me patch into the Phoenix 216 and listen in on Carpathia."

"What's going on?"

"Fortunato is itching and scratching. He acts like something bit him. Even Carpathia is laughing about it."

Judd scratched his head. "I can't remember, is there some kind of plague of mosquitoes or something on its way?"

"I'm not sure either, but watch out for Carpathia's grand entrance."

"What else is going on?"

"They've got a new guy, Loren Hut. I think he's the new head of Morale Monitors. He says every one of them is carrying a weapon there in Israel, and all the rest will be armed around the world by the end of next week. And get this, Nicolae is expecting opposition."

"He'd better," Judd said. "There's plenty of it. And not just from Christ followers."

"This guy gets more evil every time I hear him. He's telling his head guys how to kill anyone who opposes him. He wants people to suffer before they die. And even after they've been killed, he wants them beheaded as an example to others."

"Are they headed this way?"

"Yes, they will be leaving within ten minutes. They have been going over the schedule, changing things."

"Changing what?" Judd said.

"Believe it or not, they are planning a mockery of the last steps of Jesus to Golgotha."

"I believe it."

"Carpathia cut out half of the stuff they had planned. He said it never happened. The others protested, said it was part of tradition, but Carpathia just cut it."

A chill went down Judd's spine. Carpathia was claiming to have been present when Jesus was mocked, spit on, and nailed to a cross. Judd knew Jesus would win the final victory. He would crush Satan and all of his followers in three and a half years. That was one triumphal entry Judd hoped he would live to see.

Darrion had slept a few hours off and on during the kids' ordeal in Iowa. With help from Melinda, Janie, and Becky Dial, they had monitored incoming e-mails, news from the Global Community's Web site, and any other information they could find.

Now, with everyone asleep in the underground shelter in Wisconsin, Darrion wandered into the media room. She was encouraged about the safe return of the kids and the escape from the Iowa GC facility. Jim Dekker was safe, and The Cube had reached many around the world.

But there were also problems and question marks. How would the kids survive for three and a half years without taking the mark? How many believers would lose their lives standing up to Carpathia?

Darrion recognized Commander Kruno Fulcire on Global Community Network News. An anchor had broken into the live coverage in Israel to highlight something happening in the States. Mark walked in and Darrion asked him to record the interview.

"And when did this occur?" the news anchor said.

"We finished the interrogation about an hour ago and gave the prisoner an opportunity to obey international law," Fulcire said. "He refused, so we immediately implemented punishment."

"The guillotine?"

"The loyalty enforcement facilitator, yes."

"What kind of information did you get from this Pete Davidson?"

Darrion gasped.

"It's surprising how much this truck driver knew," Commander Fulcire said. "He gave us names of Judah-ites, locations of hideouts and storage facilities. He even told us where Judah-ites are hiding weapons of mass destruction."

"The guy's lying," Mark said.

"How do you know?"

"First, Pete would never have talked, and second, since when do the Judah-ites have weapons of mass destruction?"

The news anchor continued his questioning. "So the Judah-ites plan actions against the Global Community?"

"Of course. It's what they live for. They want to disrupt the peace and harmony the Global Community has tried to create. Davidson was one of their low-level operators, with a very small intellect. You see, these people are easy to lead. They're brainwashed by these religious crazies and they choose death over taking the mark of loyalty."

The screen switched to a live shot of crowds in Jerusalem.

"Before we continue with our live coverage from Israel, sir, just one more question. We've heard of a Global Community Morale Monitor deciding not to take the loyalty mark. Is there any truth that there are more Judah-ites working inside the Global Community?"

Fulcire hesitated. "We do have some reports which haven't been confirmed yet that I can't go into. One that I can mention is the case of Morale Monitor Claudia Zander. She is missing from her post in Des Plaines."

A photo of Claudia flashed on the screen along with a special hot-line number.

"We are in the early stages of developing rewards for those we suspect of being Judah-ites," Fulcire continued, "but now we simply want to talk with this Morale Monitor and make sure she hasn't fallen into the wrong hands."

"Think we should wake the others?" Darrion said.

Mark shook his head. "Pete's dead. They'll find out in the morning. I'm worried about this Zander girl. We all assumed she was faking being interested in the message. Have you checked e-mail lately?"

Darrion had been concentrating so hard on the broadcast that she had forgotten the Web site. There were at least a hundred more messages since she had checked it.

"There," Mark said, pointing to an e-mail with the subject line, *Help!*

Darrion opened it quickly and saw the message was from Claudia.

> *Dear Young Trib Force,*
> *They were going to make me take the mark, so I ran like you suggested. I grabbed a few things from the apartment, and I took*

Natalie's Bible. I guess that was okay since she's gone.

I need a place to hide until I figure out what to do next. This new commander is really intense. I don't know if you heard, but the guy in Iowa chose the blade. I don't think I could ever stand up like that, but I guess God could give me the courage.

I'm sorry for rambling. Please e-mail or call me as soon as you can. I'll put my number at the bottom of this message.

And one more thing. I still can't see the mark Dr. Ben-Judah wrote about. Does that mean I'm not a true Judah-ite?

Darrion scribbled Claudia's phone number on a scrap of paper and saved the message. "Do you think we should wake Vicki?"

Mark looked at his watch. It was almost time for Carpathia to make his grand entrance in Jerusalem. "She needs to know about Claudia. Wake her."

Judd dialed Chang and apologized for bothering him. "It's no bother," Chang said. "I'm a multitasker. Mr. Hassid has me back on track."

"What did he say?"

"He chewed me out and said I don't have time to focus on my dual marks. He even threatened to destroy the setup he and I worked so long to build, so I'm going to concentrate. When I have time, I'm going back to find video recordings of what really happened when I got Carpathia's mark."

"Let me know as soon as you do," Judd said. "Things are heating up here. There's more excitement down the street."

"Nicolae is on his way. I've heard the image of Carpathia is being moved to the Temple Mount. People are gathering there to worship it and take the mark of loyalty."

"It's time for a showdown," Judd said.

"Just keep away from the cross fire," Chang said. "And keep praying that the undecided choose Christ!"

TEN

Carpathia's Triumphal Entry

JUDD walked through one of the ancient gates of Jerusalem and nearly lost sight of Lionel and Sam, all three pushed by the huge crowds bustling toward the city. Judd watched for Chaim Rosenzweig and Buck Williams, but the place looked like a human sea. Lionel and Sam caught up with Judd, and the three prepared for Carpathia's arrival.

Thousands cheered in anticipation. Toddlers were held high on shoulders, waving real palm branches. Teenagers wearing Z-Van's style of clothes danced through the streets, forming a human chain. Many of them already had the mark of Carpathia and celebrated by shouting slogans and singing songs.

"I wonder if Z-Van is going to make an appearance at this," Lionel said.

"You can bet he's ticked if he doesn't get to," Judd said.

Judd's heart leapt when a loudspeaker truck moved through the street announcing that all citizens were expected to display the mark of loyalty to Carpathia. "Why not take care of this painless and thrilling obligation while His Excellency is here?"

A teen in the line of dancers shouted, "Come on, we're going to the Temple Mount now to get our mark!" Several people followed, but most stayed, not wanting to miss a glimpse of Carpathia.

Lionel glanced at Judd, his eyes wide. "You think they're going to check and see if we have the mark?"

"Relax," Judd said. "Those application facilities have to be packed."

People sang an off-key song a block away. Judd finally realized it was "Hail Carpathia." Hundreds broke into wild applause, thinking Nicolae had appeared. A GC tank topped with revolving blue, red, and orange lights rolled past. Behind that was a motorcade of three black vehicles, followed by more tanks. The crowd cheered and Judd hustled for a better view.

When the convoy stopped, another cheer

rose. The first black vehicle held local and regional dignitaries. They exited, quickly followed by the Most High Reverend Father Leon Fortunato. Leon straightened his long robe, then slowly scratched at his hip.

Judd explained what Chang had overheard about Leon's pain. Sam wondered if this was part of the next plague sent by God. Global Community officials Suhail Akbar and Walter Moon stepped from the second car, but the biggest ovation yet came when a woman dressed in blue stepped from the vehicle. Her white hair stood out among all the men dressed in dark suits. Though she was short, she carried herself regally, her head held high and her back straight. She moved to a podium and held up both hands. The crowd hushed as she leaned toward the microphone.

"Who's that?" Lionel said.

"Isn't she a relative of Nicolae?" Judd whispered.

"It's Viv Ivins," a woman behind them said. "She's a member of the potentate's inner cabinet." The woman eyed the three boys. "Why haven't you taken the mark of loyalty?"

Judd smiled and moved a few steps away. "Guess we have to be more careful."

Viv Ivins welcomed the participants and introduced honored guests. When she welcomed "our spiritual leader of international Carpathianism, the Reverend Fortunato," the crowd went wild. Judd noticed that Leon was still scratching his backside.

Judd recalled Sabir's imitation of "Hail Carpathia" as Leon led the crowd, directing with his right hand and scratching with his left. Voices echoed off buildings, and people had a difficult time staying in sync with each other.

As Leon urged the throng to "sing it once more as we welcome the object of our worship," an official opened a door and Nicolae Carpathia bounded out alone and bowed deeply. The crowd gasped, then roared in approval as they saw Carpathia's gold sandals, glistening white robe, and glowing, silver belt. Nicolae stretched out his hands toward the crowd, as if he were ready to embrace them all, as a group of bodyguards dressed in black suits formed a half circle behind him.

A military truck pulled up and Judd noticed a strange smell. Looking closely at the trailer hitched to the truck, Judd saw a dangling rope and two enormous eyes.

Sam drew close to Judd and whispered,

"Here it comes. The moment I have been dreading."

It took Vicki a few minutes to awaken from her dead sleep. She hobbled into the meeting room groggy and half awake, but one glimpse of the scene on television and her eyes were open.

Nicolae Carpathia looked like some kind of Greek god with bad jewelry. If the scene wasn't such a shake of the fist at God, it would have looked funny. The camera showed a trailer ramp lowering and two Peacekeepers leapt inside. Another angle caught them pulling and pushing something off the truck.

"Is that what I think it is?" Vicki said.

The two Peacekeepers struggled with a massive pig, trying to pull it onto the street. The camera angle switched and showed Nicolae Carpathia gazing at the enormous animal.

"Look at the size of that thing!" Darrion said.

"I don't think I can watch," Vicki said.

Mark flipped a switch to record the scene and turned. "We need to tell you about Claudia."

Judd watched in fascination and revulsion as the pig walked a few more steps and stopped. A leather saddle was fastened around its middle, complete with stirrups. The animal seemed woozy, unaware of the crowd's whooping and yelling. Though GC handlers had scrubbed the pig clean, the stench almost took Judd's breath away.

"They must have drugged it," Sam said, "but why?"

They soon found out. Carpathia waved at the crowd, pointed at the pig, and laughed. When he reached it, he cupped the pig's face in his hands and draped a noose around its neck.

"He's going to ride it?" Lionel said.

"That's why they drugged it," Judd said. "Under normal conditions that pig would never let anyone on its back."

Carpathia grabbed his robe, pulled it up to his knee, and got onto the pig's back. The crowd laughed and hooted as Carpathia jammed his feet in the stirrups and yanked on the rope, ordering the pig down the street.

"Why wouldn't they use a horse?" Lionel said.

"He's putting all religions in their place,"

Sam said, "especially Jewish and Christian religions."

"That's right. Jews don't eat pigs," Lionel said.

"And since Christianity comes out of the Jewish faith, Carpathia offends two groups with one ride."

Judd looked back at the gathering of dignitaries near the microphone and noticed that Leon Fortunato was still scratching.

Vicki ran a hand through her hair and checked the clock. It was a little after three in the morning. Making life-threatening decisions with this little sleep was dangerous, but if Claudia was telling the truth, they had to help.

"Driving back there could be suicide," Mark said.

"What if we find out where she is," Darrion said, "and let someone who doesn't know her go in?"

Vicki heard someone move behind her and turned. Manny Aguilara waved sheepishly and said, "I'm sorry. I woke up and couldn't help hearing. Let me do it. Claudia doesn't know me."

Vicki looked at Mark. "Let's talk. And,

Darrion, write Claudia and ask her exactly where she is."

As Darrion typed, Vicki took a breath and prayed for wisdom.

Judd followed Carpathia and was joined by Sam, Lionel, and thousands of spectators lining the Via Dolorosa. People sang and cheered Nicolae as the pig carried him along. Suddenly, the drugged animal pitched forward, its front legs buckling, and a few aides helped the potentate off.

The crowd became too thick to move through, and Sam suggested they go another route to Calvary. "I think he'll eventually go there."

They arrived at the traditional site of Jesus' crucifixion and took their place at the base of the hill. Carpathia arrived a few minutes later, climbed to the edge of the Mount, and threw his arms out.

Leon Fortunato stepped beside Nicolae and imitated him, still scratching his rear. "Behold the lamb who takes away the sins of the world!" Fortunato roared.

Suddenly, the sky blackened and Judd felt a gust of wind. People murmured and looked for shelter, but Fortunato seemed to anticipate their movement. "You need not move if you are loyal to your risen ruler! I have been imbued with power from on high to call down fire on the enemies of the king of this world. Let the loyalists declare themselves!"

Thousands screamed and waved in support of Carpathia. Judd looked around for any other believers, wondering if Chaim Rosenzweig would stand to challenge the evil one.

The sky was black as night and Judd could only see Fortunato when lightning flashed. "Today you shall have opportunity to worship the image of your god! But now you have opportunity to praise him in person! All glory to the lover of your souls!"

People around Judd knelt and raised their arms in praise to Nicolae. Judd recognized what a dangerous position he and his friends were in. They were not about to bow the knee to Carpathia or his statue. Would they be struck dead?

"You think we ought to get out of here?" Judd whispered to Lionel and Sam.

Before either could answer, Fortunato yelled, "How many of you will receive the mark of loyalty even this day at the Temple Mount?"

The crowd rose as one to wave and cheer. Fortunato responded with, "My lord, the very god of this world, has granted me the power to know your hearts!"

"Is that true?" Lionel whispered.

Judd shook his head. "That's not what Tsion teaches. He says Satan doesn't know what we think. How could he tell Fortunato if he doesn't know himself?"

Lightning flashed and claps of thunder overwhelmed the crowd. "I know if your heart is deceitful!" Fortunato yelled. "You shall not be able to stand against the all-seeing eye of your god or his servant!"

People began singing "Hail Carpathia" as Fortunato looked at the crowd with piercing eyes.

Suddenly, everyone fell deathly still as a woman a few yards from Judd screeched and pointed at Carpathia and Fortunato. "Liars!" she screamed. "Blasphemers! Antichrist! False Prophet!"

The people around her moved away quickly, and the woman was left alone. As Judd listened, he thought her voice sounded familiar.

"Woe unto you who would take the place of Jesus Christ of Nazareth, the Lamb of God who takes away the sin of the world!" the woman continued. "You shall not prevail against the God of heaven!"

Lightning flashed and Lionel grabbed Judd's arm. "That's Hattie Durham!"

Lionel was right. It *was* Hattie! Judd had first seen the woman on an airplane over the Atlantic the night of the disappearances. Though she had spent some time working for Nicolae, she was now a member of the Tribulation Force.

"I have spoken!" Fortunato spat back.

"Yours is the empty, vain tongue of the condemned!" Hattie yelled. She pointed to heaven and said, "As he is my witness, there is one God and one mediator between God and men, the man Christ Jesus!"

Judd was so captivated by Hattie's words that he didn't see Fortunato's movements. He heard a ghastly sound behind him and instinctively ducked as a ball of fire roared from the sky, lighting the whole area.

Hattie Durham didn't have time to react. She burst into flames and Judd fell to the ground, shaking, screaming, scared out of his mind. Sam and Lionel huddled close, their eyes covered. Judd wondered if they would be next.

Judd peeked at Hattie once more and saw fire engulfing her body. She seemed to melt in the white-hot heat, her body shrinking to the ground. The sun appeared again, chasing the darkness. A soft breeze blew Hattie over, and Judd noticed her shadow imprinted on the ground.

The crowd focused on Fortunato. "Marvel not that I say unto you, all power has been given to me in heaven and on the earth!" he said.

Carpathia slowly led the procession away from the area. Some people in the crowd kicked at Hattie's ashes or spit on her remains. When most of the crowd was gone, Judd knelt beside Hattie and thanked God for a courageous woman who dared stand up to the most evil ruler the world had ever seen.

ELEVEN

Nicolae's Claim

Judd caught his breath and told Sam how he had met Hattie. He wished there was something he could do for her.

"Do you want to go back to Yitzhak's house?" Sam said.

Judd nodded. "I think I'd better. Seeing that happen to someone you know . . ."

Lionel put a hand on his shoulder. "We understand. We'll give you a full report when we get back."

As Judd walked through the oncoming crowd, he wondered about Operation Eagle and when Rayford Steele and the other pilots would airlift believers and Jews out of Jerusalem. What a massive job that had to be. And with an enemy like Carpathia, it was vital that they get these people out before Carpathia killed them.

Lionel and Sam moved with the crowd toward the Garden Tomb. By the time they arrived, Supreme Commander Walter Moon was speaking.

"Oh, he's better than all right, judging by his performance at Golgotha," Moon said.

"Who's he talking about?" Lionel said.

"Shhh," an older woman in front of Lionel said. "Reverend Father Fortunato has gone ahead for preparations. Please be quiet."

Sam looked at Lionel and frowned. "Everything's ready at the Temple Mount. Why would he leave?"

Vicki explained Claudia's situation to Manny and he perked up. "I might be able to help."

"How?" Vicki said.

"There may be someone in the gang who could do this for us, but you have to understand that the people we're dealing with don't think like you. We'll have to motivate them."

"Give them something?" Vicki said.

"Exactly."

Vicki looked at Darrion. "How much money do we have left?"

"A few hundred Nicks," Darrion said.

"Is there anybody inside the gang who owes you?" Mark said.

Manny bit his lip. "There is one person. His name is Hector."

"Call him as soon as we hear where Claudia is," Mark said.

Judd sat heavily on a couch in Yitzhak's basement. Mr. Stein and the other witnesses were spread out in Jerusalem. The images of Hattie Durham flashed through Judd's mind. He dialed Chang, but there was no answer.

A few minutes later Chang called back. "I was on another call, and you will not believe what I have found."

"You won't believe what I've just seen," Judd said. He detailed the episode at Calvary and what had happened to Hattie.

Chang said he had seen the event on the live GC feed. "I was on the phone with Mr. Williams. He is there in Jerusalem with Chaim. We've just discovered top secret information about Fortunato. He is being treated by one of the palace doctors for some kind of rash. They report that it looks like boils erupting from his skin."

"That would explain why he's scratching so

much," Judd said. "Was that why you were so excited when I called earlier?"

"I have more good news, but let me share it with you later."

Lionel and Sam moved for a better view of the Garden Tomb. The afternoon sun was hot, and Lionel was glad when Nicolae stepped from behind a curtain. The crowd before him didn't cheer or sing. They seemed afraid and many had chosen to go straight to get their mark instead of watching Carpathia's evil spectacle.

"I was never entombed!" Carpathia began. "I lay in state for three days for the world to see. Someone was said to have risen from this spot, but where is he? Did you ever see him? If he was God, why is he not still here? Some would have you believe it was he behind the disappearances that so crippled our world. What kind of a God would do that?"

Lionel glanced at Sam and whispered, "This whole show is supposed to mock Jesus."

"I stand here among you, god on earth, having taken my rightful place," Carpathia said. "I accept your allegiance." He bowed and the crowd applauded.

Walter Moon stepped forward and bent toward the microphone. "He is risen!"

"He is risen indeed," the crowd replied, less than enthusiastic.

Moon chided them and the crowd responded a little louder. "We are providing you with the opportunity to worship your potentate and his image at the Temple Mount, and there you may express your eternal devotion by accepting the mark of loyalty. Do not delay. Do not put this off. Be able to tell your descendants that His Excellency personally was there the day you made your pledge concrete."

Moon lowered his voice and added, "And please remember that neither the mark of loyalty nor the worshiping of the image is optional."

The wind whipped up as a helicopter landed to take Carpathia and other dignitaries to the Temple Mount. Lionel saw many with the mark heading for the holy site, while others rushed to get in line for their mark.

While Vicki waited for Claudia's response, the kids watched the live coverage in Jerusalem. Darrion called the others over when she found an e-mail from Tsion Ben-Judah. Vicki could tell by the way he composed the message that the man's heart was heavy.

I received a message from our sister in Christ, Hattie Durham, composed two days ago. As she was praying in her hotel room in Tel Aviv, God sent the angel Michael to minister to her. He said he had come in answer to her prayers.

Michael encouraged her to be strong and said, "Those who turn many to righteousness shall shine like the stars forever and ever. Many shall be purified, and made white and refined, but the wicked shall do wickedly; and none of the wicked shall understand, but the wise shall understand."

Hattie believed she should speak out against the lies of the Antichrist. She knew there were others who had been believers longer and asked why she should be chosen to confront the evil one. In her note she said, "Maybe this is all silly and will not happen. If I chicken out, it will not have been of God and I will intercept this before it gets to you. But if you receive it, I assume I will not see you until you are in heaven. I love you and all the others, in Christ. Your sister, Hattie Durham."

Hattie was the one who spoke against

*Carpathia and his False Prophet Leon
Fortunato. She was consumed by fire, but
we will see this dear sister again.*

Vicki sat stunned. She remembered her
conversation with Hattie years before, trying
to convince her that the Bible was true and
giving her life to God was the only choice.
Now Hattie was dead, another casualty in the
war between good and evil. Vicki wondered
when all the dying would end. She put her
head in her hands and wept.

Lionel and Sam moved cautiously toward the
loyalty application facility and the brewing
chaos. Hundreds of military vehicles were
parked outside the Old City. Sam wanted to
avoid them, but Lionel noticed only a few
Peacekeepers tending the vehicles. When
they came near the Temple Mount, Lionel
saw why. Global Community personnel
were in line to take the mark themselves.
Citizens who rushed to be processed grew
angry that they had to wait in the back of the
line.

Sam led Lionel to the Wailing Wall where
many Orthodox Jews were praying. "These
men, even if they are not believers in

Messiah, will oppose the defiling of the new temple."

As Peacekeepers and Morale Monitors took the mark, Lionel and Sam moved to the east-facing steps of the new temple. It sparkled in the sunlight, a replica of Solomon's original temple. As they approached, Sam pointed out the image of Carpathia, an exact replica of the man. People fell to their knees when they first glimpsed the golden statue, some crying or singing softly. Then they quickly moved on and dozens more fell to their knees.

A dark cloud covered the sun and the temperature dropped suddenly. The huge crowd fell silent as the golden statue seemed to rock back and forth. Then a deep voice boomed from the image. "This assemblage is not unanimous in its dedication to me! I am the maker of heaven and earth, the god of all creation. I was and was not and am again! Bow before your lord!"

Lionel froze. If the image shot fire like Fortunato, he and Sam were dead. He didn't want to kneel before the image, but his legs felt shaky.

"Don't look at it," Sam whispered. "Just move away slowly."

Lionel kept his head down, but the voice again blasted behind him. With every word he expected a bolt of lightning or an explosion of fire to engulf him.

"The choice you make this day is between life and death! Beware, you who would resist the revelation of your true and living god, who resurrected himself from the dead! You who are foolish enough to cling to your outdated, impotent mythologies, cast off the chains of the past or you shall surely die! Your risen ruler and king has spoken!"

Lionel had made it to the outer edge of the crowd and was glad to be alive. He turned and looked at those in line for the mark. More and more pilgrims took their place behind GC personnel.

"Carpathia's right," Sam whispered. "This is life or death, but those people have no idea they're choosing death."

Lionel had seen enough. He and Sam quickly made their way through the streets back to Yitzhak's house.

Vicki watched in horror as GCNN covered Nicolae's appearance at the temple. Carpathia announced he would be watching all night until every citizen of Jerusalem had received the mark of loyalty and worshiped his image. "And tomorrow at noon, I will ascend to *my* throne in *my* new house."

Darrion yelped and said they had a new message from Claudia. Vicki turned from the scene of Nicolae waving farewell to the crowd and studied the e-mail.

> *I'm sorry it took me so long to get back to you. If you'll tell me when to expect you, I can arrange to be at a nearby restaurant, if you'd like. I'm at a hotel, but I only have enough money to stay one more night. Please call me or come get me.*
>
> *Claudia*

Vicki looked at Mark. "What do you think?"

"She gave us a phone number and location. That's a good sign."

"She seems sincere," Darrion said, "but it could still be an act."

"We can't afford to not take her seriously," Vicki said.

Manny called his friend Hector. After a few minutes of conversation, Manny hung up.

"What did he say?" Vicki said.

Manny hesitated. "Hector said he would help us find out if Claudia is telling the truth. We should go now."

TWELVE

Murder in the Holy Place

VICKI called a meeting of the Young Trib Force in Wisconsin. The underground hideout was overcrowded with new arrivals, and everyone knew some would eventually have to move to another hiding place. Vicki explained the situation with Claudia and, though there was intense discussion, they agreed that Mark and Vicki would accompany Manny back to Des Plaines in hopes of bringing Claudia to safety.

Vicki stressed the importance of prayer, and everyone agreed there would be someone in a designated room praying while they were gone.

"We've received another message from Dr. Ben-Judah," Vicki said.

"Nobody else has died, have they?" Charlie said.

"No. This is a message he wants everyone to hear. I'll leave it for you to read, but I want to stress a couple of his points.

"Tsion says Nicolae has scheduled what the Bible calls the desecration of the temple." Vicki pulled an Old Testament text onto the huge screen. "Daniel prophesied that the king of this time period in history will 'exalt and magnify himself above every god' and 'shall speak blasphemies against the God of gods.' "

"What are blastomys?" Charlie said.

Vicki smiled. "A blasphemy is making fun of God. It means you take what is holy, and make it unholy. It's like riding a pig down the Via Dolorosa just to make fun of Jesus."

Charlie nodded. "That Carpathia's a really bad guy."

"Tsion writes about why people don't believe the truth of God. There is a danger that the people we're trying to reach have hardened their hearts. People who do this won't be able to change their minds."

"But we don't know who those people are," Darrion said.

"Exactly," Vicki said, "so we need to keep giving the message and looking for as many opportunities as possible."

When she was through, Mark, Manny, and Vicki knelt in the middle of the room. Jim

Dekker and Colin Dial prayed first, putting their hands on them. The others prayed and asked God to protect them when they began their travels later that night.

Judd awoke wondering if it would be his last morning on earth. It was clear Carpathia and Fortunato had the power to kill believers, and with all the GC Peacekeepers and Morale Monitors in Jerusalem, Judd knew he had to be careful.

He walked with Mr. Stein toward the Temple Mount. Sam and Lionel followed a few minutes behind. Military vehicles lined the streets leading to the Old City, but there were few Peacekeepers or Morale Monitors.

Mr. Stein smiled. "The Global Community workers are experiencing the truth of the Bible."

"I don't get it," Judd said.

"Revelation 16:2 says, 'So the first angel left the Temple and poured out his bowl over the earth, and horrible, malignant sores broke out on everyone who had the mark of the beast and who worshiped his statue.' "

"A plague of boils?"

"Yes."

One of Mr. Stein's friends rushed to them.

"It's happening. The prophet of God has come!"

"Where?" Mr. Stein said.

"At the Temple Mount. He just spoke and demanded an audience with the evil one. He warned Carpathia not to touch the remnant of Israel, believers in Jesus of Nazareth! He calls himself Micah. And when Global Community guards tried to shoot him, they became paralyzed. Now one of the GC leaders is questioning Micah."

Judd and Mr. Stein rushed toward the Temple Mount, finally spotting a ring of GC Peacekeepers around an old man dressed in a monklike robe. The robe was gathered at the waist by a braid of rope.

The GC leader identified himself as Loren Hut and ordered people to stand back. A television camera caught the action as Hut pulled a gun from its holster, scratched himself, and prepared to fire at the man named Micah.

The gun exploded so loudly that the crowd fell back. Expecting to see a lifeless, bloody body, Judd opened his eyes to see Micah alive and well. Loren Hut fired again, only inches away, but again the bullet appeared to miss. Hut fired the gun again and again, but nothing happened.

Someone near Judd laughed and said,

"This is a joke! A put-on! He's shooting blanks!"

Loren Hut screamed, "Blanks?" He turned and fired directly into the man's chest. The man fell backward, dead before he hit the ground. Hut turned and fired two more shots at Micah, but neither did any harm. Hut threw his gun away and rubbed his body against a nearby tree, crying in agony.

Minutes later Carpathia arrived by helicopter. He approached the gathering and made sure cameras were trained on his every move. Judd and Mr. Stein stood behind the scene a few yards but could hear every word spoken.

"You are too old to be Tsion Ben-Judah," Carpathia said. "And you call yourself Micah."

Judd saw contempt on Carpathia's face. As Judd studied Micah, he thought it could be Dr. Chaim Rosenzweig, but he wasn't sure.

After one of Carpathia's troops fell to the ground scratching and writhing in pain, Carpathia said, "I concede I have you to thank for the fact that nearly my entire workforce is suffering this morning."

"Probably all of them," Micah said. "If they are not, you might want to check the authenticity of their marks."

"How did you do it?"

"Not I, but God."

"You are looking into the face of god," Carpathia said.

"On the contrary, I fear God. I do not fear you."

"So, Micah, what will it take for you to lift this magic spell that has incapacitated my people?"

"There is no magic here. This is the judgment of almighty God."

Nicolae smiled. "All right. What does *almighty God* want in exchange for lightening up on this *judgment?*"

For the next few minutes Judd watched as God's servant dealt with the evil ruler. Finally, Micah said, "A million of God's chosen people in this area alone have chosen to believe in Messiah. They would die before they would take your mark."

"Then they shall die!"

"You must let them flee this place before you pour out revenge on your enemies."

"Never!"

Judd looked around and realized everyone who had Carpathia's mark was now either on the ground writhing in pain or moving to makeshift medical tents for help.

"Your only hope to avoid the next terrible plague from heaven is to let Israelis who believe in Messiah go," Micah said.

Carpathia's eyes darted back and forth. "And what might that next plague entail?"

"You will know when you know," Micah said. "But I can tell you this: It will be worse than the one that has brought your people low. I need a drink of water."

Someone brought a bottle of water, and Micah showed Nicolae it had turned to blood.

Nicolae said, "I want my people healthy and my water pure."

"You know the price."

"Specifics."

"Israeli Jews who have chosen to believe Jesus the Christ is their Messiah must be allowed to leave before you punish anyone for not taking your mark. And devout Orthodox Jews must be allowed a place where they can worship after you have defiled their temple."

Judd's mind reeled. He was watching prophecy fulfilled before his very eyes. Carpathia left, and people who had not yet taken the mark volunteered to help set up cameras and equipment. As they followed Micah to the temple, Judd noticed Mr. Stein's lips moving in silent prayer.

"Citizens!" Micah said in a clear voice. "Hear me! You who have not taken the mark of loyalty! There may still be time to choose to obey the one true and living God! While the evil ruler of this world promises peace, there is no peace! While he promises benevolence and prosperity, look at your world! Everyone who has preceded you in taking the mark and worshiping the image of the man of sin now suffers with grievous sores. That is your lot if you follow him.

"By now you must know that the world has been divided. Nicolae Carpathia is the opponent of God and wishes only your destruction, regardless of his lies. The God who created you loves you. His Son who died for your sins will return to set up his earthly kingdom in less than three and a half years, and if you have not already rejected him one time too many, you may receive him now.

"You were born in sin and separated from God, but the Bible says God is not willing that any should perish but that all should come to repentance. Ephesians 2:8-9 says that nothing we can do will earn our salvation but that it is the gift of God, not of works, lest anyone should boast. The only payment for our sins was Jesus Christ's death on the cross. Because besides being fully man, he is fully God and his one death had the power to cleanse all of us of our sin.

"John 1:12 says that to as many as received him, to them he gave the right to become children of God by believing on his name. How do you receive Christ? Merely tell God that you know you are a sinner and that you need him. Accept the gift of salvation, believe that Christ is risen, and say so. For many, it is already too late. I beg of you to receive Christ.

Vicki sat in the backseat as Mark drove through the night. Manny said he could feel the prayers of the people in Wisconsin. Manny tuned in nonstop radio reports from Jerusalem and around the world about the plague of sores that affected everyone who had the mark of Carpathia. Even news reporters were in pain.

He found one station that aired a live broadcast from New Babylon featuring Dr. Consuela Conchita. Her voice was strained as she suggested people bathe often and wear loose clothing.

Mark shook his head. "It's going to take more than soap and baggy pants to stop this plague."

Lionel and Sam drew close to Micah as dozens of unmarked civilians approached the old man and prayed with him. Immediately the mark of God's seal appeared on their foreheads.

Micah rose to speak. "Those of you who are Jews, listen carefully. God has prepared a special place of refuge for you. When Carpathia's plans to retaliate reach their zenith, listen for my announcement and head south out of the city. Volunteers will drive you to Mizpe Ramon in the Negev. My assistant here will tell you how to recognize them by something we can see that our enemy cannot. If you cannot find transportation, get to the Mount of Olives where, just as from Mizpe Ramon, you will be airlifted by helicopter to Petra, the ancient Arabian city in southwestern Jordan. There God has promised to protect us until the Glorious Appearing of Jesus when he sets up his thousand-year reign on earth."

"Praise God," Sam whispered as he looked over the crowd. "I wish Daniel was here to hear this."

"Maybe he is," Lionel said.

As the time of Nicolae's appearance at the temple neared, Orthodox Jews approached. Micah pleaded with them to believe the truth about Jesus, but they scowled.

Finally, Carpathia arrived, arguing with Micah and the holy men and telling them they would know soon that he was god. He threatened Micah, then turned to the Orthodox Jews. "You will regret the day Israel turned her back on me. A covenant of peace is only as good as either side keeping its word."

"Boo!" an Orthodox man shouted and others joined in. "You would dare blaspheme our God?"

Carpathia turned toward the temple, then spun back. "Your God? Where is he? Inside? Shall I go and see? If he is in there and does not welcome me, should I tremble? Might he strike me dead?"

"I pray he does!" a rabbi shouted.

Carpathia glared at the men. "You will regret the day you opposed me. It shall not be long before you either submit to my mark or succumb to my blade."

Lionel glanced at one of the huge monitors strategically placed for all to see and noticed the network feed showed Carpathia going inside the temple. Outside, men cried out to God.

Now it was Micah's turn. He raised his voice for all to hear. "If you are God, why can you not heal your own Most High Reverend Father or the woman closer to you than a relative? Where are all your military leaders and the other members of your cabinet?"

Carpathia walked back outside and Micah

continued. "Where are your loyal followers, those who have taken your cursed mark and worshiped you and your image? A body covered with boils is the price one pays to worship you, and you claim to be God?"

Nicolae finally went inside again, and Lionel noticed the feed had switched to GCNN in New Babylon. The news anchor explained Carpathia's movements and gave a brief history of the battle over who should be worshiped in the temple. "His Excellency will eventually enter the Holy of Holies," the newscaster said, "but first he is insisting on the removal of the dissidents. Let's go back."

Lionel shuddered as Carpathia appeared in a darkened inner chamber of the temple. "Anyone not here in honor to me may be shot dead," he said. "Are you armed and prepared?"

"No!" someone said.

Another man said, "I am armed."

"You," Nicolae said, pointing to the first man, "take Mr. Moon's weapon and do your duty."

The camera turned and showed the face of the man refusing the gun. Sam gasped and said, "It's Daniel, the man I introduced to you yesterday! He must have volunteered so he could be close to Nicolae."

But Daniel refused the gun. The camera

shook and a shot rang out. Someone cried in pain. The camera locked on Carpathia holding the gun. He nodded in the other direction and said, "Show him." The camera panned and Lionel spotted Daniel's body, still and lifeless.

Lionel felt sick to his stomach. Carpathia had killed Daniel without hesitation. Had Daniel refused because he saw who Nicolae really was? Was there a chance he could have become a believer?

Suddenly, the video feed showing the body switched to a close-up of Micah. His voice boomed through the speakers on the monitors overhead.

"Not only does the evil ruler of this world want to rid the priests of their rightful place in their own temple," Micah said, "but it also appears he has personally committed murder at this holy site."

Lionel put an arm around Sam as the boy wept. Lionel knew the world would get violent in the next few years, but how much worse could things get?

About the Authors

Jerry B. Jenkins (www.jerryjenkins.com) is the writer of the Left Behind series. He owns the Jerry B. Jenkins Christian Writers Guild, an organization dedicated to mentoring aspiring authors. Former vice president for publishing for the Moody Bible Institute of Chicago, he also served many years as editor of *Moody* magazine and is now Moody's writer-at-large.

His writing has appeared in publications as varied as *Reader's Digest, Parade, Guideposts*, in-flight magazines, and dozens of other periodicals. Jenkins's biographies include books with Billy Graham, Hank Aaron, Bill Gaither, Luis Palau, Walter Payton, Orel Hershiser, and Nolan Ryan, among many others. His books appear regularly on the *New York Times, USA Today, Wall Street Journal,* and *Publishers Weekly* best-seller lists.

Jerry is also the writer of the nationally syndicated sports story comic strip *Gil Thorp,* distributed to newspapers across the United States by Tribune Media Services.

Jerry and his wife, Dianna, live in Colorado and have three grown sons.

Dr. Tim LaHaye (www.timlahaye.com), who conceived the idea of fictionalizing an account of the Rapture and the Tribulation, is a noted author, minister, and nationally recognized speaker on Bible prophecy. He is the founder of both Tim LaHaye Ministries and The PreTrib Research Center. He also recently cofounded the Tim LaHaye School of Prophecy at Liberty University. Presently Dr. LaHaye speaks at many of the major Bible prophecy conferences in the U.S. and Canada, where his current prophecy books are very popular.

Dr. LaHaye holds a doctor of ministry degree from Western Theological Seminary and a doctor of literature degree from Liberty University. For twenty-five years he pastored one of the nation's outstanding churches in San Diego, which grew to three locations. It was during that time that he founded two accredited Christian high schools, a Christian school system of ten schools, and Christian Heritage College.

Dr. LaHaye has written over forty books that have been published in more than thirty languages. He has written books on a wide variety of subjects, such as family life, temperaments, and Bible prophecy. His current fiction works, the Left Behind series, written with Jerry B. Jenkins, continue to appear on the bestseller lists of the Christian Booksellers Association, *Publishers Weekly, Wall Street Journal, USA Today,* and the *New York Times.*

He is the father of four grown children and grandfather of nine. Snow skiing, waterskiing, motorcycling, golfing, vacationing with family, and jogging are among his leisure activities.

The Future Is Clear

Check out the exciting Left Behind: The Kids series

Books #31 and #32 coming soon!

Discover the latest about the Left Behind series and complete line of products at

www.leftbehind.com

Hooked on the exciting
Left Behind: The Kids series?
Then you'll love the dramatic audios!

Listen as the characters come to life in this theatrical
audio that makes the saga of those left behind
even more exciting.

High-tech sound effects, original music,
and professional actors will have you
on the edge of your seat.

Experience the heart-stopping action and
suspense of the end times for yourself!

Three exciting volumes available on CD or cassette.